D1281762

THE UNEXPECTED WEDDING

KAY CORRELL

ROSE QUARTZ PRESS

Published by Rose Quartz Press

090516

ISBN: 978-1-944761-08-0

This book is dedicated to my father, lost in his Alzheimer's world.
Dad, I miss you so much.
#freepoppy

KAY'S BOOKS

Find more information on all my books at *kaycorrell.com*

COMFORT CROSSING ~ THE SERIES
The Shop on Main - Book One
The Memory Box - Book Two
The Christmas Cottage - A Holiday Novella (Book 2.5)
The Letter - Book Three
The Christmas Scarf - A Holiday Novella (Book 3.5)
The Magnolia Cafe - Book Four
The Unexpected Wedding - Book Five

The Wedding in the Grove - (a crossover short story between series - with Josephine and Paul from The Letter.)

LIGHTHOUSE POINT ~ THE SERIES
Wish Upon a Shell - Book One
Wedding on the Beach - Book Two

Love at the Lighthouse - Book Three

INDIGO BAY ~ A multi-author sweet romance series
Sweet Sunrise - Book Three
Sweet Holiday Memories - A short holiday story

Sign up for my newsletter at my website *kaycorrell.com* to make sure you don't miss any new releases or sales.

CHAPTER 1

B ecky Lee Tesson tucked a pencil behind her ear and glanced at the tall man walking into the Magnolia Cafe. His gaze roamed the restaurant, looking it over, or looking for someone, she wasn't sure. The stranger moved to one side of the doorway and a small boy, about seven or so, stood by his side.

Keely, the owner of the cafe, led the duo to a table by the window. The boy trudged behind the man and slipped into a chair without the bounce and energy she'd come to expect from being around her friend Bella's seven-year-old son. The sunlight streamed through the window and highlighted the little boy's curly blonde hair. Both the man and the boy wore jeans and t-shirts. The boy's t-shirt said Tigers Baseball, but Becky Lee had no idea who the Tigers were, not a team from around here.

Becky Lee dropped off a check at a customer's table and headed over to get the man and boy's order. She threaded her way through the tables to the front of the cafe and smiled at the pair as she approached. The little boy looked up at her with bright blue eyes that looked red and swollen from tears. Her heart tugged with an instinct to try to make it better for him. Something nagged at her, too, but she couldn't put her finger on it. The boy looked vaguely familiar, but she couldn't place him. It was like she knew him, but she didn't.

Still trying to figure it out, she turned back to her job. "Afternoon. I'm Becky Lee. What can I get for you two?"

The man stared at her name tag, lingered a bit too long looking at her face, then pulled his gaze away. "We'll take two burgers, fries, and vanilla shakes. Does that sound good to you, kiddo?"

The boy bobbed his head.

"Coming right up." Becky Lee took their menus and headed to the kitchen. She would swear she could feel the man's eyes watching her as she walked away.

Don't be crazy.

She waited on a few more tables while the man's order was being cooked. Each time she glanced his direction it seemed like he was watching her. It's not like she was immune to a good-looking guy's attention, but an uneasy feeling swept over her, and she always listened to her gut.

"Keely, do you know that guy and little boy by the front window?" Becky Lee walked behind the counter and leaned closer to Keely.

"Nope. Never seen them before. Why?"

"Not sure. Just wondering."

"Is there a problem?"

"No, I'm just being silly." Becky Lee headed to the kitchen to pick up their order.

Cal couldn't help staring at Becky Lee. She did look familiar, but then he'd assumed she would. She was pretty and efficient and had a quick smile. A smile that he knew and remembered so well.

The heaviness descended on him again, but he did his best to push it away. He looked over at Scotty. The boy was staring silently out the window, poor kid. Cal was clueless on how to help him. He'd tried, but nothing he'd done had helped. He'd heard the boy cry himself to sleep last night... not that he blamed him. Cal was dangerously close to tears himself, but he refused to give in to them. He had too much to do, too many responsibilities. As much as he felt he was sinking in quicksand, he had to find his footing, had to sort things out.

Becky Lee came over, arms laden with their delicious looking, albeit not quite healthy meal.

"Here you go. Ketchup's on the table. Do you like ketchup on your fries?" Becky Lee smiled at Scotty.

Scotty looked up at her with his wide blue eyes and nodded.

"You guys going to be around for a bit? We're having a big picnic and fundraiser in the city park this weekend. Should be fun. Lots of activities for the kids. We had a tornado come through here a bit ago. We're trying to raise some money to help out some of the businesses that got hit the hardest."

"We'll be here for a while. Scotty, what do you say? Does that sound like fun?" Not that he expected something different, but Scotty just nodded.

"There's going to be pony rides and they're going to do rides down Main Street on the fire truck. Bet you'd like that." Becky Lee stood beside the table. If she was hoping for more than a nod, she was disappointed. "Hopefully, we'll see you there."

"I was wondering if you could recommend a place for us to stay for a few days."

"Sure can. Sweet Tea Bed and Breakfast. Right up Main. Run by my friend Rebecca and her husband, Larry. Good folks."

"Thanks. I appreciate the suggestion."

"No problem. Tell them I sent you." Becky Lee walked away from the table to go help another customer.

Cal leaned across the table and cut Scotty's hamburger in half. "That's how you like it, right?"

Scotty nodded again.

Well, he'd at least found a place to stay for a few days. He needed to find a job, too. Then find a place to live more permanently than a B&B. Scotty needed some stability in his life right now.

So he'd find a job, find a place to live… and stay under the radar the whole time. He'd eventually have to figure out the whole schooling situation for Scotty, but since it was summer, he was going to put that on the back burner. He smothered a sigh. Maybe the whole mess would get sorted out before then and everything would go back to normal and he wouldn't have to worry about finding a school for Scotty.

A random thought hit him like the tornado Becky Lee had just mentioned. He was going to have to find childcare for Scotty while he worked. He raked his hands through his hair. He was so out of his element. What else was he letting fall through the cracks?

Oh, and how could he forget… he still had to blow Becky Lee's whole world apart.

CHAPTER 2

Cal pulled his car up to the Sweet Tea Bed and Breakfast. The B&B was a large white house with a wide front porch. Hopefully, they'd have a room and he could get Scotty settled in. The boy looked exhausted. Maybe he'd crash early tonight and finally get some sleep.

"Come on, kiddo. Let's go see if they have a room." Cal opened the door for Scotty and they climbed the steps to the front door. A sign said "come on in," so they did.

A woman in her fifties, he'd guess, came bustling in from the back. "Hello there. Looking for a room?"

"We are. Not sure how long."

"One or two rooms?" The woman smiled at them.

"One is fine."

"I've got one with a full bed and a twin day bed. How does that sound?"

"That sounds perfect."

She led the way to a counter near the entryway while peppering them with questions and information about the town as she got them registered. He paid cash for three nights. Would it take him longer than that to find a job and a place to live? He'd no clue. The last ten years or so, he'd usually drifted from job to job without really worrying about the next one. Something always had turned up, and he'd enjoyed the freedom it had given him. He'd reveled in no longer living up to the expectations he'd been raised to believe he had to meet.

"We have breakfast here from seven to ten." Rebecca smiled at Scotty. "Do you like pancakes?"

Scotty just nodded, of course.

"Good. Well, follow me and I'll show you to your room."

Cal and Scotty followed Rebecca up the stairs to a large room on the back of the B&B. She opened the door and handed him the key. "Looks over the garden." She nodded over to a window seat then pointed to the right. "Bathroom over there. Lots of towels."

Scotty crossed the room and climbed up on the window seat.

"You let me know if you need anything."

"We will. Thank you."

He closed the door behind the woman and dropped the duffle bags to the floor. He hadn't had time to pack a lot. He hadn't really known what all to get for Scotty. He'd randomly stuffed clothes in two suitcases, a handful of his books and toys, and his ball glove and bat. That was all still loaded in the trunk of his car. He'd stuffed pajamas, jeans, and shorts in a duffle for the road trip.

He'd realized later he'd forgotten to get any other shoes except for the worn shoes the boy had on. He'd no idea when, or even if, he'd get a chance to go back and get more of Scotty's things.

"Can I watch TV?"

"You bet you can, kiddo."

The boy walked over, switched on the TV, and turned it to some kids' station. He climbed onto the bed, flopped on his stomach, and settled in to watch the show.

Cal walked over and looked out onto the garden below. Tomorrow he'd job hunt. He'd have more money if he could access his accounts, but he didn't think that was a smart idea at this point. He'd taken a wad of cash… a big one… before he left. Should be enough to tide them over a bit, put down a deposit on an apartment, and pay for some childcare while he worked to get some more money coming in.

The heaviness came again and he sank down on the window seat. Sometimes it was too hard to fight. He gave into it this time and wallowed in his grief.

Cal chased Scotty into a shower the next morning amid a litany of complaints. The boy came out scrubbed and clean with his wet hair plastered to his head and fresh, if wrinkled, clothes on. Getting this kid into the shower and new clothes seemed like one of the hardest jobs he'd ever attempted. Cal was feeling kind of proud of himself for his success when he and Scotty headed downstairs to breakfast. The coffee scent had been taunting him since he'd first awakened.

Rebecca greeted them as they entered the dining room. "Morning. Hope you slept well. I'm getting ready to make up another batch of pancakes. Coffee is over there on the sidebar, and orange juice, too, if you want some. I'll be back in a few minutes with your breakfast."

Scotty slid into one of the chairs and fiddled with the silverware. Cal gratefully walked to the sidebar and poured a steaming cup of black coffee and took a sip. *That's what I'm talking about.*

"Want some OJ, kiddo?"

"Yep."

Cal was pleased that Scotty had at least moved onto one-word answers. Maybe he was dealing with the shock a little better. Maybe.

A man entered the room with a newspaper tucked under his arm. "Morning. I'm Larry, Rebecca's husband. You must be our new guests."

Cal walked over and shook the man's hand. "Cal." He nodded at the boy. "And Scotty."

"Pleased to meet you both. What brings you to town?"

Cal froze. He didn't know what to say or how to explain. He cleared his throat. "Just looking for a change."

"Well, Comfort Crossing is a nice little town. Friendly people. Safe. Good schools." Larry set the paper down on the table. "You got a job lined up?"

"Not yet." Cal sucked in a quick breath. So much to do and get sorted out.

"What kind of work do you do?" Larry poured himself a cup of coffee and took a sip out of the mug.

Cal didn't even know where to start. He'd done so many things over the last years. Waiter, mechanic—he'd been lousy at that, managed a small shop, and did some construction work. "Construction work." Cal figured he'd go with that. It didn't really matter to him what he did now, he just wanted some money coming in until things settled down.

"Tell you what, I heard that Steve Bergeron was looking for some more workers. He owns his own construction company. Going gangbusters these days. New construction as well as repairs from a tornado that came through town a bit ago. I could hook you up with him."

"That would be great." Cal had really enjoyed his construction work, seeing things built with his own hands. He'd enjoyed the framing as well as the woodwork and thought he'd been pretty good with it.

"I'll give him a call and tell him I'm sending you over to talk to him."

"I'd really appreciate that."

Rebecca came in with plates of pancakes, bacon, sausage, and a bowl of fresh fruit. Cal laughed out loud when he saw Scotty's plate. Rebecca had made the boy's pancakes into shapes. An S for Scotty—or maybe it was a snake? And a sorry-looking puppy face.

Scotty's face lit up. "Those are for me?"

"I'm not too good at the shapes, but I thought I'd try. Cal gets the boring old round kind."

"Thank you, ma'am." Scotty dug into his pancakes.

Rebecca turned to her husband. "I heard you talking about Steve Bergeron?" It was half statement, half question.

"Yes, Cal here is looking for work. Going to send him over to talk to Steve."

"Great idea." Rebecca turned to Cal. "I was talking to Holly—that's Steve's lady friend, our new veterinarian in town—and she said that Steve was really shorthanded and looking for good, reliable workers."

"I can really use the work and I have construction experience."

"Well then, hope it works out for both of you." Rebecca turned to head back to the kitchen. "You let me know if you want more pancakes."

CHAPTER 3

Becky Lee sat at the Magnolia Cafe with her friends Jenny and Bella. Well, she was Bella to the townsfolk, but to the trio of friends, she was Izzy—short for Isabella.

They'd finished up breakfast and still sat catching up on their lives. "I'm glad you two could come in this morning before my lunch shift. I've missed you two newlyweds. How's the whole marriage thing working out?"

Jenny set down her coffee cup. "There's been some adjustments. Moving in with Clay. Combining the kids so there're three kids under one roof. But I'm glad to be married to the man. Finally."

"Only took you, what? About twenty-ish years since you first met him?" Becky Lee loved how her friends' eyes shone when she talked about Clay. "How about you, Izzy? Things going well with you and Owen? Jeremy coming around any?"

"Owen and Jeremy are slowly finding their footing with each other. Who knew a ten-year-old boy could cause so much turmoil. The funny thing is, I think he likes Owen, he's just afraid to admit it. But Owen is really patient with him. Timmy, of course, is nuts about Owen. They are quite the pair." Bella pushed her plate away. "I hope that we get to go on that honeymoon we planned. It just wasn't possible right after the wedding. Everything was crazy here in town after the tornado with too much going on, but we didn't want to wait to get married."

"Well, your double wedding was beautiful. I can't imagine anything better than seeing my two friends married to guys they are obviously in love with. Not to mention that Owen is crazy in love with you, Izzy. And, of course, Clay has been in love with Jenny since high school. So you both had a fairy tale ending."

"I've got some other news." Bella looked at her friends and a wide grin spread over her face. "We haven't told anyone else—I wanted you two to be the first. We're going to have a baby."

"Seriously? That's wonderful." Jenny jumped up and hugged Bella.

Becky Lee sat for a moment, a bit stunned. She had no idea that Bella and Owen were planning on having children. A momentary twinge of jealousy coursed through her, but she immediately stomped it down. She reached across the table and squeezed Bella's hands. "I'm so happy for both of you."

"Owen is in shock, I think. A bit overwhelmed with

the whole being a father thing. I told him he has months to get used to the idea."

"He'll come around." Jenny grinned. "This is fabulous news."

"We told the boys this morning, so I wanted to tell you first thing because they are probably blabbing the news to everyone at their day camp, so the whole town will know soon."

"I'm tickled for you. You do look radiant. Is that why you've had like two sips of your coffee? You never do like coffee much when you're pregnant, and you didn't order bacon. Man, we should have figured this out. Those are your two tells when you're pregnant." Becky Lee smiled at her friend. "You feeling okay? You had a bunch of morning sickness with Jeremy and Timmy."

"I feel right as rain. Never better."

"Hope it stays that way for you this time." Jenny sat back down in her seat.

"Me, too. Life is a bit crazy now with Owen moving into the carriage house—at least when he's in town—and the shop getting busy with the summer tourist season. I love living in the carriage house, it's so convenient having it right behind the shop, but Owen is talking about buying some place a bit bigger for all of us. I just don't know. The boys have had so many changes."

"The carriage house only has the two bedrooms. It will be quite the squeeze after the baby is born." Jenny crinkled her brow. "You could use that sunroom as a nursery, I guess. It would be a tight fit though."

"I know. I do think we'll need to move. If we do, then Owen could have an office at the house, too. I know he really wants that. It's just a lot of changes."

"He's probably right that you should move." Becky Lee knew her friend loved the carriage house, but it really was too small for a growing family. "I bet he'll find you something you'll love."

"I'm sure he will. I know he's been looking. He said when he finds the perfect place, he'll show me to make sure I like it. I've been looking at houses online, but I barely have enough time to breathe right now, much less traipse through a bunch of houses, so he's doing all the beginning legwork on it."

Becky Lee stood up. "I better go get all set for work before the lunch crowd gets here. Izzy, I'm really happy for you."

"Thanks, Bec."

"I'll see you guys soon." Becky Lee headed to the storage room off the kitchen to get her server apron and get ready to start her shift.

Bella watched her friend walk away from the table. She turned to Jenny. "I almost felt bad telling Becky Lee about being pregnant. I know she's always wanted kids. I'm sure she's happy for me, but still, I know it must be hard for her."

"I'm sure it is. I just wish she'd find someone as wonderful as Owen or Clay. She deserves it. I think it's been years since she's even dated someone for more than a handful of dates."

"Well, she knows what she likes, always has. She's never going to settle for anything else."

"Sometimes what we *think* we need and is exactly right for us is different from what is really best for us."

Bella laughed. "Like me and Owen. Never would have thought that one would work. He's all fancy businessman from a big city, I'm a shop owner in a small town."

"Yet, look how it all worked out."

A wave of gratitude washed over Bella. She sometimes couldn't believe how lucky she was. She and Owen did seem to be the perfect fit now—even if they came from totally different backgrounds. She placed her hand on her belly. Now she was having his baby.

A smile slipped across Jenny's face when she noticed the hand on the belly movement, the one so many women had done for so many centuries. "Owen is in for another new experience in a few months."

"He is. He's excited, but I actually saw a bit of fear mixed in with it. He's just getting used to living with my rowdy two, and now we'll add another into the mix. I think he's afraid he won't be a good father. He sure has nothing to pattern fatherhood after."

"It does sound like his father was a cold man."

"You mean because he basically shipped Owen off to boarding school his whole life? Or how he refused to acknowledge Jake was his son?"

"Owen is nothing like that. You can see how hard

he's worked at gaining your boys' trust. I don't think he's anything like his father."

"He has been great with the boys. I'm sure he'll be great with this new little one."

Bella looked across the restaurant and saw Becky Lee watching them. She smiled at her friend, but self-consciously slipped her hand off her belly.

CHAPTER 4

Cal pushed through the door to Steve Bergeron's construction company with Scotty following closely behind him. A man looked up from the table he was standing behind and smiled. "You must be Cal. Larry called and said he was sending you my way. I'm Steve."

Cal crossed the room and shook the man's offered hand. A firm handshake. He could always tell a lot about a man from his handshake.

A small boy came running from a room off to the side followed closely by an Australian shepherd dog. They both skidded to a stop beside Steve. "Hi, I'm Josh. This is Louie." He turned to Scotty. "What's your name?"

"Scotty." Scotty leaned over and patted the dog. The dog thumped his tail in response and wriggled in excitement.

"Dad, can I go show Scotty the fort I'm making out back?"

"If it's okay with Cal."

Cal had no idea what was okay and what wasn't these days, but if Scotty wanted to go with the boy, and it took the haunted look from his eyes, he was good with that. Cal nodded.

Scotty, Josh, and Louie headed out the back door of the office.

"We can keep an eye on them out the window." Steve nodded towards the back window. "Now, Larry says you have construction experience. What have you done?"

"I'm great with drywall, done a lot of the framing, too. I've done tiling and wood floors. I've also done quite a bit of painting and I'm a bit of a perfectionist with it."

"That sounds great. I'm so shorthanded these days. I do run background checks on all the people I hire."

Cal froze. Of course, he'd do that. There would be paperwork to fill out, a social security card to show.

Steve looked at him, one eyebrow arched in a question. "Is there a problem? Something a background check will turn up?"

"No. Well, yes. I mean." Cal raked his hands through his hair. "I go by Cal Gray. But you'll see when I do the paperwork, it's not my given name. I'd prefer to still be known here in town as Cal Gray, though."

"Are you in some kind of trouble? I can't have trouble around my son or my company."

"It's… a family thing."

"Ex-wife?"

"No, nothing like that. I just need time to sort it out. You can do a web search on my real name and you'll find out… things. I'd prefer to stay under the radar right now."

"As long as the background check goes well, I'm fine with calling you whatever name you want."

"And if you can keep what you find out private, I'd appreciate that."

"I can do that. If it all checks out, when can you start?"

"Whenever you want. I need to find a place for Scotty and me to live. We're staying at the Sweet Tea in the meantime. And I need to find childcare for Scotty."

"Tell you what. If you want to go in the back with the boys and help with that fort they're building, I'll run my checks. I'm badly in need of help, so we'll get you started as soon as you can sort all that out."

"Here is my driver's license with my given name."

Steve took the license. "I'll run the check."

"That sounds great." Cal headed toward the backdoor. "You'll see I check out. It's just… complicated right now."

Steve's eyes widened when he ran a quick check on Cal's given name and found out who he really was. It seemed strange a man from that background would take a construction job, but it sounded like he'd done it before. Steve glanced out the window and saw Cal nailing a board on Josh's ever-growing ragtag fort he was building behind the office.

Steve usually had good instincts when it came to people, and his gut was telling him to hire Cal. He didn't know why Cal was keeping his real identity a secret, but the man must have his reasons. There wasn't any legal problem that came up, so his inclination was to hire the man.

He made one quick phone call before talking to Cal.

Cal came back in the office when Steve called out the window.

"You checked out like you said. I'm sure you have your reasons for lying low. That's fine with me. None of my business as long as it doesn't affect your job." Steve handed Cal a slip of paper. "Here's my cell phone number, and the pay rate. I think it's a fair wage for the area."

Cal glanced and the paper and nodded. "Thank you. I appreciate you giving me a chance."

"Another thing. My neighbor, Mrs. Baker, watches Josh for me most days during the week. I called her cell, and she's willing to watch Scotty, too. She's a very reasonably priced sitter, and said it would be nice for Josh to have a friend to play with."

Steve could see the relief in Cal's eyes.

"I can't thank you enough for the job and the help with finding someone to watch Scotty." Cal crossed the room and shook Steve's hand. "You've done so much for me, for us. I won't let you down."

"I hope not because it looks like our sons have become fast friends."

A look of… something… flashed through Cal's eyes. The man was probably overwhelmed with things falling into place. Steve knew how hard it was to raise a boy by yourself. If he could make things a bit easier on Cal and Scotty, then it was the right thing to do.

Steve wrote the address of his house and handed it to Cal. "Tell you what. I'll meet you at my house tomorrow about noon. I'll introduce you to Mrs. Baker, she should be back from church by then. You can start work on Monday."

"Thank you. I'll see you tomorrow, then."

Steve settled down at his desk to do some of the never-ending paperwork for his company. He looked up later when the door opened and sunlight came streaming inside on the old wooden floorboards. Someone stood in the doorway, blocking the light.

"Holly." He came from behind the desk and wrapped his arms around her. She stood on tiptoe and kissed him.

"I missed you. I had a break in my schedule and thought I'd pop in and see you. Are we still on for dinner tonight?"

"We are. Josh already has the table set up all fancy. He wants to pick flowers from the garden, too."

Holly's face crinkled into a warm smile. "He sure is getting into this fancy dinner thing."

"He is. Says it's good to have a woman in the house. The kid cracks me up."

"You know, you two don't have to go to all this trouble when you invite me over."

"We're just so dang happy you moved to town."

Steve nuzzled her neck. "I'm particularly happy to have you here."

"Hmmm. I'm kinda glad I moved here, too." She leaned into his embrace.

The back door flew open and Josh burst in. "Hey, Miss Holly. You're here."

"I am."

"Did Dad tell you I already set the table for dinner? You didn't change your mind did you? You're still coming?"

"Wouldn't miss it."

Josh grinned from ear to ear.

"I better get back to work. Gil Amaud found a stray dog hanging around the Feed and Seed, looking for food. He followed her and found a litter of puppies. Looks like someone abandoned her and the pups. He's bringing them in to let me check them out."

"That's cool. Can I come see them too?"

"It's up to your father."

"Can I, Dad? Please? I won't get in Miss Holly's way. I promise."

"Okay, but come straight back here after that. Don't go getting in the way over there at the vet clinic."

"I don't get in the way. I'm a big help when I'm there, aren't I, Miss Holly?"

"You are. Come on. Let's see what you can help with until Gil shows up with those pups."

Steve watched Holly and Josh walk down the street toward the veterinary clinic. Josh skipped around and popped back from side to side around Holly. The boy had more energy than ten people.

Steve smiled then, content with his life. Josh was happy, Holly had moved to Comfort Crossing, and things were working out between them. Good. Better than good. He was nuts about the woman, but knew she needed some time to adjust to all the changes in her life the last few years. But he'd give her time. All the time she needed.

Becky Lee looked up to see that man from yesterday and the little boy—*Scotty, wasn't it?*— coming through the door to the cafe for a late lunch. The man still looked a little too closely at her, like he was searching for something.

Or, of course, it could be her imagination.

"Grab a seat anywhere. I'll be by in a sec to get your order."

The man picked up two menus from the counter by the door and headed over to a window seat. Scotty looked perkier today, and for some reason that tickled her. She never could stand to see a sad child, it tore at her heartstrings.

She brought over the order for Sue Lake, a history teacher at the local high school. The woman smiled up at her. "I sure do like my summers. Late lunches at the cafe. No papers to grade. I bet I've read fifty books so far this summer."

Becky Lee laughed. "Just like the school kids. Everyone enjoys their summers."

"I'm reading an entire series of romances set in the

Scottish highlands. The author did a remarkable job with the historical details."

"Sounds right up your alley." Becky Lee set the plates on the table. "Let me know if you need anything else."

"I will."

Becky Lee watched as the woman propped a book open beside her lunch and started reading. With a quick glance around the cafe, she didn't see anyone else who needed her attention, so she headed over to the man and Scotty.

"Good to see you again."

"Thanks."

"Did you get all settled at the Sweet Tea?"

"We did. Thanks for the recommendation."

"Can I have a grilled cheese?" The little boy looked up at her with bright blue eyes. They reminded her of someone, but she couldn't quite connect the dots.

"You sure can. We make a great grilled cheese here. How about some fries with that?"

"Yep. And a shake. I can have a shake, can't I?" Scotty looked at the man across from him.

"Sure thing. And I'll have the meatloaf sandwich."

"Another good choice. Comes with a salad."

"Ranch dressing, please." The man handed her the menus.

"It'll be up in a flash." Becky Lee took the menus and walked away, determined not to spin around to see if he was staring at her.

Cal watched Becky Lee walk away. She had some familiar mannerisms. The way she cocked her head to the side when she asked a question. A dimple on one cheek that wrinkled when she smiled. So familiar. He looked across at Scotty and saw him watching Becky Lee. Surely the boy hadn't noticed. Maybe. He was pretty certain Scotty didn't miss much and was wise beyond his years.

He needed to talk to her, but without Scotty hearing the conversation. He wasn't sure how he was going to pull that off.

The door to the cafe opened and Steve and Josh stood in the doorway. He saw Josh talk to Louie, and the dog sat down outside the entrance. "I'll be back after we eat. You stay here, Louie." The boy followed his father inside. He tugged on his father's hand. "Hey, Dad. Look. Let's go eat with Scotty."

They came over and Cal invited the two of them to sit. Becky Lee came and took their orders, and the boys talked nonstop through lunch. Well, Josh talked constantly, and Scotty joined in here and there. But at least Scotty was talking instead of just yes-no answers or slight nods. That was an improvement.

"Dad's taking me to the park next. Have you been to the park? It's cool. It's got swings, and a merry-go-round and a fort. We could get my soccer ball out of Dad's truck. Do you play soccer? I do. I'm good at it, aren't I Dad? You wanna come, Scotty?"

Scotty looked at Cal.

"We could do that." Cal turned to Steve. "I really need to talk to Becky Lee for a few minutes first."

"How about I take the boys on over to the park, and you join us there when you're finished?"

Relief washed over Cal, that would work. He'd have a chance to talk to Becky Lee without Scotty overhearing. "Thank you."

They paid their bills, and Steve headed out with the boys. Cal sat at the counter until Becky Lee rang out the last customer from the lunch crowd.

"Becky Lee. How much longer is your shift?"

"Why?"

"I need to talk to you."

"What about?"

"I'd rather wait until you're finished here."

He could see the unease in her eyes. "I need... to talk to you."

"You're acting all mysterious."

"It's important. Really important. I just need a bit of your time."

"We can talk here."

"I mean privately."

"Not to sound suspicious or anything, but I don't even know you. Why do you need to talk to me, and why privately?"

He drew in a deep breath. She had a point. He sounded like a crazy stalker. He thrust out his hand. "Cal Gray."

She shook his hand but then pulled back. "So, Cal Gray, nice to meet you. Now, what did you want to talk about?" She stood firmly planted behind the counter.

"Look, it would really be better somewhere... private."

"It will have to be here."

"I just… listen… it's about your sister."

Becky Lee eyed him suspiciously. "Which one?"

"TJ."

"Theresa Jean?"

"Please. Can we talk?"

Becky Lee looked closely at him for a long moment and he shifted uneasily, not entirely sure she'd agree to talk with him. She finally nodded. "Okay. We'll grab a table in the back." She turned to another young woman. "Keely, I'm going to take my break now, that okay with you?"

Keely came behind the counter. "Sure. I'll finish up the after-lunch chores. Take your time."

Becky Lee turned to him. "Back this way."

They headed towards the back of the cafe and he squared his shoulders, readying himself to give her the news.

CHAPTER 5

An uneasy feeling pulsed through Becky Lee as she led the way to a back table. She sat down across from Cal. He was obviously about as nervous as she was. The muscle at his jawline twitched slightly and he clenched and unclenched his fists, even though he was seemingly oblivious to the gesture. "Well, what is this about Theresa Jean?"

"It sounds strange to hear her called that. I mean, I know that's her given name, but I've always known her as TJ."

"Well, I've never known her as TJ, but when you called her that... well, she's the only sister with those initials, it wasn't a big leap. I haven't heard from her in over eight or nine years. She got into a row with Pops and left town. She always was a stubborn, independent person. I thought she'd come back eventually. Or at least contact me or one of my sisters. Do you know where she is now?"

"I… um… yes, I do."

"I think you need to just get to the point."

"I have some news about your sister."

"You're killing me slowly here." Becky Lee pinned him with her best cut-to-the-chase stare.

"She's been in an accident."

Becky Lee sat up straight. "Is she okay? Where is she?"

"She's okay. No." Cal shifted uneasily in his seat. "Well, she's in a coma. She's been in one for about three weeks now."

A pang of regret and guilt stabbed Becky Lee. She should have tried harder to find her sister after she left. She'd always figured Theresa Jean would come home when she was ready. She hadn't been that close to her younger sister. They had a ten-year age difference and were worlds apart in personalities, but that was no excuse. "How—what happened?"

"It was a car accident. She survived but then needed surgery a few days later. She's been in a coma ever since."

"I need to go see her. Where is she?" Becky Lee's heart wrenched in her chest.

"That's the thing. Right now the best thing for her is to *not* go see her."

"You're talking crazy. Of course, I need to go be with her. Talk to her. See if I can make her wake up."

"Please, listen for a minute. That's not what she wants. We talked before the surgery. Things are complicated. My brother—her husband—died in the crash."

Becky Lee saw the raw pain in Cal's eyes. "Theresa Jean was *married*?"

"Yes. To my brother. They were so... happy. The perfect couple." Sorrow flashed through Cal's eyes. "This whole thing is... awful."

"I'm sorry about your brother." It seemed the right thing to say to him but so not enough. She was sorry a man had died. A man *married* to her sister. A man she hadn't even known existed. Her thoughts whirled and she leaned forward. "So, tell me why I can't go see my sister."

"Because she wants you to stay here and help take care of your nephew."

Her heart caught in her throat and she sat in dazed silence.

"I have a nephew?" Becky Lee sat across from him, a stunned look on her face, one hand resting at her throat.

"Yes. Scotty."

"Scotty is my nephew? I thought he was your son?"

"No, he's my nephew, and as you can imagine he's reeling from all the changes in his life."

"Why aren't you and Scotty with Theresa Jean?"

"Still feels weird to hear you call her that. You two look so much alike. Same smile, some of the same mannerisms. She's like a brunette version of you." Cal knew he was stalling. It was time to tell her just how complicated things really were.

Becky Lee sat silently with her head cocked to one side, waiting for an answer to her question.

"She asked me to come here with Scotty if anything happened." He paused not sure how to say it and soften the blow. "In case… she didn't make it."

Becky Lee flinched.

"I don't think either of us considered she might survive the surgery but not wake up. I stayed there as long as I dared, thinking she'd come out of the coma, wanting to be there for her. I talked to her. Scotty talked to her. But she wouldn't come around. Eventually, I knew I had to take Scotty and leave."

"I don't understand that. Why would you leave her all alone like that?"

"To keep Scotty safe." Cal leaned forward on the table. "It's a long story, but the short version is that we need to hide him for as long as we can."

"Hide him?" Becky Lee's brow crinkled. "From whom?"

"My father."

"Your father? His grandfather? Why does he need to be hidden from him?" Becky Lee's mind was swirling with questions. Where was Theresa Jean? How did all this happen? How could she not know that her sister was married? She had a son for Pete's sake. A son. "You need to explain this to me."

"My father tried to take Scotty away from her before. That's not something anyone would want for their child, to be raised by my parents. Trust me on that."

From the serious, wrinkled forehead and the clench of his jaw, Becky Lee had no reason to doubt him.

"But how could they take him away from Theresa Jane and your brother?"

"My brother was… away… for a while."

"He left her?"

"No, it wasn't like that."

"What was it like?"

She watched him clench his fist and open it along with his now telling twitch of his jaw muscle. She waited for him to continue.

"He was in prison."

Becky Lee sat back in her chair, pretty sure she couldn't handle even one more shocking revelation today. Or ever for that matter. She cringed before she had the courage to ask, "What did he do?"

"White collar crime. He was gone—in prison—for eighteen months. My parents sued for custody while he was gone. Said your sister wasn't fit. They had the money for good lawyers. Great lawyers. Your sister—well, I helped her as much as I could—but she didn't have much money. Worked long hours to make ends meet. Luckily my brother got released early and they had a stronger case to keep custody. I have no doubt my father will try again now that my brother's… gone."

"So you took Scotty and ran?"

"Seemed like the best plan at the time. Keep him hidden and give TJ time to heal and wake up."

"Do you have kids of your own?"

"To be honest, I know nothing about raising a kid. I mean, I was around Scotty some while he was growing up. Moved to TJ's town while my brother was in prison. That is the sum total of my experience. But TJ trusted me with him. I'm not going to let her down."

Becky Lee wondered how her sister could think a single guy, with no experience with kids, would be a good guardian. The corners of her mouth scrunched into a scowl. "You do have legal custody, don't you?"

"I do for now. TJ made sure of that. But let's be honest, I'd be a poor choice if there is a big custody battle. So, for now, we're going to fly under the radar. But before she went into surgery, she made me promise that if something happened, that I'd come to Comfort Crossing and get you to help me with Scotty. She said you were the best older sister ever, and you'd be able to —I don't know—guide me?"

Theresa Jean thought she was the best sister ever? All Becky Lee could remember was how Theresa Jean tagged along and Becky Lee was always telling her she was too young. What kind of sister was she anyway? She didn't even know Theresa Jane was married or had a son... or was widowed. Becky Lee's heart ached for her sister, for all she'd gone through and without the help of her family. Losing her husband, raising Scotty alone when Cal's brother was in prison, fighting for custody.

"I still want to go see her."

"I'm sure my father has already found out what happened by now or he will soon. He'll have her room watched. He's that kind of man. You could lead them right back to here. Please. I promised TJ I'd keep Scotty safe and away from my parents. Will you help?"

"Of course, I'll help in any way I can." She looked out the window for a moment, trying to gather her thoughts, but they were scattered across the breeze that had picked up outside. She noticed storm clouds gathering in the sky. Ever since the tornado, storm clouds had made her jumpy. She stood up. "We should go get Scotty. It looks like we might be getting a late afternoon storm. We should tell him about me, too, shouldn't we?"

"Well, that's another thing. I think it would be better if we didn't. The fewer connections we have to your sister, the better. At least for now. Most people assume he's my son. If it gets around that you're his aunt, it's one more clue for my father to find us."

Becky Lee didn't like that, but she could see Cal's point. "Okay. For now, anyway."

Becky Lee went over to talk to Keely for a few minutes, then met him at the door. "I asked off for tonight. I need some time to absorb all this. She's calling in someone to take my shift."

Cal opened the door and they headed outside. The sun was firmly tucked behind a bruise-gray cloud. They hurried towards the city park but ran into Steve and the boys before they made it there.

"Storm coming in. I figured I'd better get the boys

back inside." Steve glanced up at the sky. "I don't trust storms much these days."

"I hear you on that." Becky Lee glanced upwards, too.

"I think we'll head out and ride out this storm at home." Steve turned away then looked back over his shoulder. "I'll see you tomorrow, Cal."

"Okay. Thanks."

Becky Lee's glance roamed over Cal, searching for answers.

"Steve gave me a job and found a sitter for Scotty. Going to meet her tomorrow and start the job on Monday."

"Steve's a good man to work for. You do construction?"

"Some. A little here and there."

"I can help out with Scotty. Watch him around my shifts. I'll talk to Keely and see if we can sort out my schedule."

Scotty looked up at Cal, his eyes wide. "So strangers are gonna watch me?"

"I've gotta work, kiddo. We've got to find someone to babysit you while I do. Josh's neighbor will help out some, and Miss Tesson will help, too."

"I'm too old for a babysitter."

"Okay, someone to keep an eye on you." Cal hid a smile.

Scotty eyed Becky Lee. "You know how to take care of kids?"

"I'm pretty good at it." Becky Lee nodded gravely.

Scotty scowled. "Are you fun?"

Becky Lee's laugh danced on the humid air. "Yes, I think I am. I've watched my younger siblings, and I've taken care of my best friends' kids. I do the fun stuff, then send them back for the hard stuff." Becky Lee winked.

"Well, Josh and me are gonna play ball when I'm with that sitter lady. What am I gonna do when I'm with you?"

"We'll find fun things. I promise."

Scotty let out a long sigh. "Okay."

Cal reached out and touched Scotty's shoulder. "Come on, kiddo. Let's head back to the Sweet Tea before the rain hits."

Becky Lee stopped him. "How about you two come over tonight for a homemade supper? I bet you're tired of eating out all the time. It will give Scotty and me some time to get to know each other better before I start baby—*keeping an eye on him* for you."

"I'll take you up on that." Cal was grateful for not only the dinner but the help with Scotty. He should have a chance to get to know his aunt, even if he couldn't know she was his aunt right now.

Becky Lee took out a piece of paper from her purse and wrote down her address. "Six o'clock sound good?"

"We'll be there."

He watched as Becky Lee hurried off down the street with a few wayward glances towards the gathering clouds.

A few big drops of rain splattered down around them. "Come on. Let's hurry up before we get caught in the rain."

CHAPTER 6

Becky Lee heard the front door open and Jenny's voice. "Bec? You here?"

"Back here."

Jenny came into the kitchen as Becky Lee put a pan of lasagna into the oven and turned around. "What are you doing here?"

Jenny plopped down in a kitchen chair. "You sounded upset when I called. Or something. Just not like yourself. I have this feeling that something is wrong and you're not telling me."

"No. Everything is fine." Becky Lee dropped the hot mitt on the counter.

Jenny eyed her closely. "Nope. Won't work. Something's wrong."

There really was no use trying to keep a secret from either Jenny or Bella. They'd always weasel it out of her.

"It's a long story."

"Well, pour me a glass of tea and get talking. And who are you cooking that big pan of lasagna for?"

"Ah, Jenny. So much has happened."

"Since this morning?"

"Well, I just found out." Becky Lee went and grabbed a glass and poured her friend some sweet tea. "It's about Theresa Jean. She's in trouble."

"You've heard from her? It's been years. What kind of trouble?"

"For starters, she's in a coma." Becky Lee could feel the tears starting to pool in her eyes. She dashed them away. There was too much to do. Too much to sort out.

"Oh, Bec. I'm so sorry. What happened? Where is she? You haven't heard from her in so long. How did you find out?"

Beck Lee held up a hand. "One thing at a time." She sank onto a chair across from Jenny, glad to have someone to talk to. "Her brother-in-law came to town to tell me. His brother—her husband—was killed in the accident."

"Oh, no. I'm so sorry." Jenny's eyes narrowed. "Wait, she was married?"

"Yes, and there's more. Theresa Jean has a son. Scotty. He's here, too. And… well, they are kind of in hiding."

"I don't get it."

"It's all confusing, but her brother-in-law is here and I'm going to help him with Scotty. Give Theresa Jean time to heal and, hopefully, come out of her coma. But for now, we're not telling anyone he's my nephew."

Jenny put down her glass of tea. "You've lost me."

Becky Lee told her the whole story while Jenny listened intently.

"I'm so sorry all this happened to your sister. And you can't even go see her? That is tough."

"It is. I want to go see her so badly and talk to her. Try to get her to come around. But Cal—that's her brother-in-law's name—says it's too dangerous. But to answer your question about the lasagna—which you asked ages ago—I'm having Cal and Scotty for dinner tonight. I want to get to know my nephew."

"Is there anything I can do?"

"I don't think so. Well, yes, can you tell Izzy what's going on? There's no use pretending I can keep a secret from you two. But make sure you don't tell anyone else. It's safer if people don't know I'm Scotty's aunt. For now."

Jenny stood up, pulled Becky Lee to her feet, and gave her a long, I'm-here-for-you hug.

"I'll keep Theresa Jean in my thoughts. I hope she recovers quickly."

"Thanks. I do, too. I feel so helpless. Cal doesn't want me to tell Pops or my other siblings, either. That's what Theresa Jean asked, so that's what I'll do for now. I can't believe all this happened without me knowing a thing. She got married. Had a son. Now she's a widow. I just…" Becky Lee grabbed a tea towel off the table, carefully folded it, and set it back down. "It will all be okay. It will. I'm going to help her now by watching her son. Help take care of him. But when she gets better? All this will change. She is not going to drift so far out of my life ever again."

"You'll have time with her soon. I know you will. Keep the faith, Bec."

Becky Lee forced a weak smile. "Yes, it will work out. Soon. She'll get better. She's a fighter."

"You call me if you need anything. Call at any time, day or night." Jenny headed toward the door.

"Thanks for coming by. I guess I didn't realize how much I needed to talk to someone. You always seem to know when I need you."

"That's what friends are for. I'll check in with you tomorrow."

"Thanks, Jenny." Becky Lee closed the door behind her friend and leaned against it. Her mind was a whirlwind of thoughts. She pushed away from the door and headed resolutely to the kitchen with firm steps. She'd feed Cal and Scotty, get to know the boy, and help Cal as much as she could.

Becky Lee had just enough time to finish preparing dinner, set the table, and change into a sundress and sandals. When she heard the knock at the front door, she glanced in the mirror in the hallway for a moment, then laughed at herself. It wasn't like this was a date. Why was she fussing so? She was nervous about hitting it off well with Scotty, though.

She crossed the front room and swung the door wide. "Come in."

Cal stepped inside, his large frame blocking the doorway momentarily. Scotty hung close to his side.

"I thought we might have some sweet tea or lemonade on the back patio while dinner finishes cooking. How does that sound?"

"I like lemonade," Scotty piped up.

Becky Lee stared at the boy for a moment, searching for signs of Theresa Jean in him, memorizing his face, wanting to reach out and hug him and tell him everything would be okay, wanting to tell him she was his aunt. But instead, she just smiled. "I made fresh squeezed lemonade. Follow me." She led them through the house to the kitchen and out onto the back patio overlooking her gardens.

"Wow, look. She's got real stuff growing back here." Scotty's voice was filled with amazement.

"I'm hoping you'll help me with my gardens when you come over."

"That would be fun." Scotty plopped into a chair. "I could do that. Mom says I'm a good helper." Silence descended on the three of them and Scotty sat still in his chair, staring at the garden. "Mom's going to get better soon. I bet she'd like to see your garden. Maybe we'll come visit you again after Mom is all better."

"I think that's a great idea." Becky Lee fought to get the words out and the tears hidden. She cleared her throat. "I'll go get the lemonade and tea."

She returned with their drinks and a jigsaw puzzle she had on hand from the last time she'd watched Bella's boys. "You like puzzles?"

"Yep." Scotty opened the box and dumped the pieces on the patio table. He carefully started searching for the edge pieces.

She and Cal sat and watched Scotty work on his puzzle. An awkwardness hung in the air between them. They made mindless chitchat about the weather and how quickly the afternoon storm had passed through leaving in its wake a cloying humidity. She was used to the mugginess, but she could see Cal wipe his forehead with a handkerchief and press the cool glass of sweet tea to his face.

"I better go in and finish up dinner." She stood up.

"Let me help. Scotty, you okay out here finishing up your puzzle?"

"Yep."

She and Cal went inside and he seemed grateful to be in the air-conditioned kitchen. "Not used to the humidity, I see."

"I better get used to it since I start the construction job on Monday."

"This is quite the heat wave we have going right now. Hopefully, it will break soon."

"Hope so." Cal looked around the kitchen. "What can I do to help? I have to admit, I'm not much of a cook. At all."

"How about getting more ice out of the freezer and filling the glasses on the table?"

"That I can do. You know, TJ used to say I'd starve if I didn't come by for dinner now and again. She's a great cook."

"Is she? I tried to teach her basics when she was growing up, but she never seemed very interested."

"Well, she must have learned, because she's an

awesome cook. She's really into healthy eating. She'd be appalled at the food Scotty has been having."

"I'm sure she'd understand that you're doing your best."

"I've always moved around a lot in the last ten years or so. Never really had a place to call home, so never had more than a pot or pan to my name. I can just load up my car and move to a new place. I eat out. A lot."

"Well then, a home-cooked meal should be a welcome change." She pulled the lasagna out of the oven and set it on the stovetop to cool. She popped some homemade rolls in the oven to heat then pulled the salad from the fridge.

"This looks like a feast to me." Cal looked at all the food with an appreciative and hungry gaze.

Becky Lee laughed. "Go call Scotty in for dinner and I'll feed you, you poor starving man. Though I'm well aware of the amount of food you put away at the cafe at lunchtime."

He grinned at her. "We growing men need our nourishment."

They ate dinner while Becky Lee spent most of the meal asking Scotty questions. If the boy was curious about why this lady was asking so many questions, he didn't show it. Cal was glad to see Scotty talking and enjoying the meal. It almost seemed... normal. Only nothing was normal at all anymore.

"Can I be excused? I want to finish up my puzzle."

"You sure may. We'll have some cookies for dessert in a bit."

Scotty pushed back from the table and started to leave.

"Take your dishes over to the sink." Cal nodded at the dirty plates, glad he'd remembered that TJ had always made Scotty clear his own place at the table after each meal. He was going to have to remember more of the rules of parenting. He didn't want to mess things up.

Scotty took the dishes and placed them in the sink, then went back outside to his puzzle.

"He seems like a good kid. Nice manners." Becky Lee watched the boy head out the door.

"He is. You should have seen him before. So full of life. Quick laugh. He and my brother… they were inseparable. My brother thought Scotty hung the moon." Cal paused for a moment to collect his thoughts. Or his feelings. Or control the overwhelming wave of loss that pounded him. But why shouldn't he feel sorry for himself? He'd lost a brother and Scotty had lost a father. And at this point, the boy had to feel like he'd lost his mother, too.

"I'm sorry I didn't get to know him before, too. Or that I never got to meet your brother."

"TJ was so into family… all about my brother and Scotty. I never could figure out why she didn't want to see her own family. But then, you must have been important to her because she asked me to bring Scotty here."

"All I know is she had a big fight with Pops. He wouldn't talk about it. Theresa Jean packed up that night and left. I didn't really even think much about it at the time. She was so fiercely independent and was always so sure she was right. I figured she'd move away for a bit, cool off, and come home. But when she didn't come home for months on end, I just couldn't figure it out." Becky Lee looked over at him, pain evident in her lapis blue eyes, the eyes so much like TJ and Scotty's. "Did she ever tell you what happened?"

"I have no idea. She just said she was estranged and left it at that."

"I've tried to get Pops to talk, but he's a closed book. About Theresa Jean. About my aunt."

"Your aunt?"

"Pops had a sister. She left town, never to be heard from again. She's passed away now though. We all got a bit of an inheritance from her a few years back. Pops won't talk about her either." Becky Lee poured herself another glass of tea and took a sip. "None of my siblings have figured out the mystery of my aunt, and none of them have heard from Theresa Jean, either."

"I'm sorry you missed so many years with your sister."

"I am, too. How about you? Were you and your brother close? Any other siblings?"

"My brother and I were close. And, yes, I have a sister. My sister is a carbon copy of my father, ruthless in business and life. She's climbing the ladder at the company." Cal rubbed his temple. "I just wish my brother would have been able to escape the hold my father had over him sooner. I will say, he never took a second look at my father or his company when he got out of prison. He and TJ moved across the country. He started over. I never believed it was Gordon who did the fraud. I think… I *know* my father threw him under the bus to protect my sister."

"So your brother took the blame for your sister?"

"The evidence all pointed to Gordon, along with my father's second in command's testimony. But my brother isn't the type to defraud anyone. I just think my brother didn't have it in him to fight it and send our sister to jail. He took a plea and got off early for good behavior. But it almost cost him his son." Cal could hear the bitterness creak through his words. How could his father have done that to Gordon, one of the kindest, most honest men he'd ever known? Though maybe that was the problem. Gordon was too honest for his father's way of life.

"I can see how you wouldn't want Scotty around a man like that."

"Father would love another heir apparent to his company. Though I'm sure Scotty would be shipped off to boarding school at the first opportunity. Then camps in the summers. That's how it's done in my family. If we were lucky, we'd get to come home for Christmas. Quite often my parents had plans, and we'd stay at our boarding schools through the holidays."

"I can't even imagine that." Becky Lee wrinkled her brow. "That's no way to raise children."

"I will do anything in my power to make sure Scotty doesn't have an upbringing like mine. I owe my brother that much. Besides, Scotty is a great kid. No way I'm going to let my father ruin that."

Cal got up to walk to the door and check on Scotty. The boy was curled up on a lounge chair, fast asleep. "I think all this has worn him out. It's been so hard on him. Losing his father. Sitting by his mother in the hospital. We had my brother's funeral without TJ. A simple burial, just Scotty and me. I didn't know if I should bring him or not. I keep worrying I'm making the wrong decisions for a kid his age."

"It was probably good closure for him."

"I had no one to ask, so I went with my gut."

"That's all you can do." Becky Lee got up and walked over to the counter. "So, where is TJ exactly?"

He paused, but he figured it didn't hurt to tell her. "She's in the medical center in Baton Rouge." He moved over to stand beside her. "TJ and my brother lived in a small town out of Baton Rouge. They loved it there."

"That close, and she still didn't come home."

He could see the pain clearly in her face and wished he could take that away. He'd seen so much pain the last few weeks, on Scotty, on TJ, now on Becky Lee. And, of course, the haunted look of pain and uncertainty was present on his own face when he looked in the mirror. He reached over and placed his hand over hers. "Maybe that's why they moved this direction. Maybe she was going to try to mend things."

"Maybe." Becky Lee's eyes clouded. "Maybe I should have done a better job trying to find her. I've looked online for signs of her, but I couldn't find anything."

"They weren't the social media types. They were trying to stay out of my father's line of sight."

Becky Lee placed her glass in the sink and turned to him. "It's all so very complicated, isn't it?"

～

"Yes, it is a bit messed up. Hopefully, TJ will wake up soon and we'll get things sorted out." Cal's eyes were filled with kindness and sympathy.

Becky Lee didn't want anyone's sympathy. She wanted to help. To do something *right now* to make things better. "I want to help her in any way I can. I hope I can persuade her to move back home to Comfort Crossing."

"I'm sure she could use the help, but she doesn't seem like the type of person to take help easily."

"No, she doesn't accept help easily. Maybe she will for Scotty's sake." Becky Lee sighed. "Listen, I want to see as much of Scotty as possible. Get to know him. Help you as much as I can."

"We need to be careful that people don't connect you two, that they don't figure out he's your nephew. We don't want them to wonder why you're spending so much time with him."

Becky Lee chewed on her bottom lip then looked directly into Cal's eyes. "I think you should date me then."

"What?" Cal's eyes widened and he pushed back from the table.

"If it looks like we're dating, no one will question if I'm spending lots of time with Scotty."

Cal rubbed his chin. "That's not a bad idea. It's a

good one, actually." He flashed a quick grin. "If we're dating does that mean we get more home-cooked meals like this one?"

A laugh bubbled up through Becky Lee. "Yes, I suppose it does. I do like having people to cook for, so it's not a problem on my part."

"Well, I guess we're dating then."

"Great, then that will give me more time with Scotty."

"Speaking of Scotty, I should get him back to the Sweet Tea and let him sleep. Poor kiddo is so tuckered out."

She watched as Cal went outside and gently scooped up Scotty as if the child would break in his arms. She held open the door and Cal walked into the house. She led the way through her home and out onto the front porch. "Thanks for coming tonight. Giving me a chance to get to know Scotty."

The boy stirred in Cal's arms and nestled his face against Cal's chest. Cal looked down with a look that said he was carrying precious cargo. He gently brushed away a lock of hair from the boy's eyes and settled him closer to his chest. The simple motion tugged at Becky Lee's heart.

She cleared her throat. "I'll look forward to our next *date*."

Cal flashed a smile and nodded.

"And call me if you need anything at all."

"I will."

She watched as the broad-shouldered man slowly walked out to his car and carefully put the boy in a booster seat in his car. Cal turned and offered a brief wave, climbed into the driver's seat, and pulled away. She watched his tail lights as he drove down her street.

Worse things could happen than spending time with a handsome guy like Cal.

She shook her head at the shallowness of the thought and turned to go back inside and clean up the dishes. Then she was going to sit down with a nice cup of chamomile tea, put her feet up, and try to sort through all the feelings racing through her. This had been the strangest day in a month of Sundays.

CHAPTER 7

Greta Miller stood on her front porch watching the sunrise. Her hands were wrapped firmly around a hot mug of coffee, the heat lessening the dull aching of her hands. The house was so quiet now that Clay and her granddaughters had moved out. She'd enjoyed having the noise and laughter and a houseful of family. She was glad her son had married Jenny, she was. It was just... soundless now. She imagined some people might enjoy the peace, and at times she did, but mostly she missed the hubbub that was family living.

She was lucky that Clay and Jenny had bought the place right down the road from her, so she did see the grandkids almost every day and could help out when needed. Though it wasn't the same as having them under her own roof.

She watched a cardinal swoop through air and land in a tree. Sometimes, in still moments like this in the early mornings, she could imagine herself as a young girl, playing in this very same front yard. She'd grown up in this house and lived all her years here. It was a part of her.

That swing in the front yard hanging from that old live oak? It had had its share of new ropes and new seats on the swing, but it still had a swing. There used to be an old picnic table under the tree, too. She and her best friend, Ellie, had spent hours under that old tree.

And Martin.

Though she rarely let her thoughts wander to Martin, or to Ellie for that matter. It was all in the past. What happened had happened and she couldn't change anything. She wasn't sure she would have changed anything even if she could. Sometimes life just gave you hard choices.

Which is probably why she, of all people, understood how Jenny had made the hard choice to keep her son, Nathan, a secret all these years. To protect him. Sometimes tough choices are made to protect the people we love. But now Clay knew that Nathan was his son, Greta had a grandson she'd never known she had, and Jenny and Clay were married. Sometimes the difficult choices turned out okay in the end.

Sometimes they didn't.

Greta took a long sip of her now cool coffee, glanced up at a hawk circling the sky, and went back inside to start her day.

Cal pulled into the driveway of Steve's house at noon on Sunday. Steve and a pretty woman with brown hair were playing croquet in the front yard with Josh. The woman laughed as she sent Steve's ball sailing to the edge of the lawn.

Josh looked up and waved. He dropped his mallet on the ground and came running up to the car with Louie racing by his side. "Hi. Come on out. Wanna play croquet?" Josh was tugging Scotty's door open.

Scotty climbed out of the car and was almost bowled over by Louie. The boy recovered his balance and turned to his friend. "I never played it."

"Come on, I'll teach you." The boys headed off across the lawn.

Steve and the woman walked up to the car. Steve had his arm loosely wrapped around her waist. "Holly, this is Cal. Cal, this is Holly Thompson. She's the vet in town."

"Nice to meet you."

"Nice to meet you. Steve tells me you're going to work for him. That's great. He's been needing some more workers."

"Glad for the job, ma'am."

"Holly. Call me Holly."

Cal nodded and glanced over at the boys. Scotty was watching Josh hit the ball with his mallet. Louie was barking and running between the two boys. Cal turned as another car pulled into the drive and an older lady got out and walked up to them.

"Mrs. Baker. Thanks for stopping by. I wanted you to meet Cal and Scotty."

"Nice to meet you, Cal."

"Boys, come over here for a minute." Steve turned and called to the boys. The boys came barreling over.

"Scotty, this is Mrs. Baker." Steve introduced the two.

Scotty stood close to Cal's side.

"Mrs. Baker is fun. She doesn't babysit me anymore. She just watches me and we do fun stuff. I'm too old for a babysitter." Josh stood tall and crossed his arms across his chest, daring anyone to argue.

"That's what I said." Scotty nodded in agreement.

"Well, good. Then I'll just watch you along with Josh. Tomorrow we're going to bake cookies, how does that sound?" Mrs. Baker's warm smile lit up her face.

"Mrs. Baker and I make the best cookies." Josh hopped from one foot to the other.

"I like to make cookies." Scotty looked up at Mrs. Baker. "What kind?"

"I'm thinking chocolate chip. Do you like those?"

Scotty nodded.

"Good. Hey, Dad, can we go back and play croquet now? I'm teaching Scotty."

"Sure thing, son." The boys ran back to play.

"I'll take good care your boy, Cal. I know it's hard leaving him with someone new. He'll have Josh to play with. I'm sure it will be fine."

Cal hoped so. There were so many decisions to make about taking care of Scotty. He hoped he was making good choices. How did a parent ever figure out all of this stuff? He was so in over his head but determined to try his best, for TJ and for Gordon.

"I'll see the boys tomorrow, then." Mrs. Baker turned and walked back to her car.

"They'll be fine with her. Don't worry." Steve waved as Mrs. Baker pulled out of the drive.

"I'm sure they will." He said it more to convince himself than anything else.

"I'm getting ready to grill out some burgers. Plenty for you two. Why don't you join us?"

Cal looked over at Scotty laughing and racing around with Josh. "I appreciate it. We'd like to join you. The boys look like they're having a great time."

"Come on then. Let's go stoke up the coals."

Steve pushed through the door with one last load of dishes from the picnic table. Holly stood at the kitchen sink, her arms plunged into soapy water, staring out the window with a smile chasing the corners of her mouth. He sometimes couldn't believe how lucky he was to have found her. She turned to him and her smile broadened. "Josh and Louie are having races."

"Josh can think of ways to make anything and everything a competition, even with a dog."

"He sure had a good time with Scotty."

"He did. I think the sitting arrangement will work out well. Give Josh someone to play with and help out Cal."

"Cal was kind of quiet during the barbecue wasn't he?"

Steve set the tray of dishes on the counter. "A lot of

changes at once for him, I guess. Moving to town, new job." He didn't want to keep secrets from Holly, but he'd respect Cal's request to be known as Cal Gray.

Steve stood behind Holly and wound his arms around her. "You don't need to be doing all that. I can clean up later." He nuzzled her neck then kissed the back of her ear.

"I don't mind. I love being out here at your house with you and Josh."

He reached up and brushed her hair away and planted a kiss on the nape of her neck.

She turned to face him and wrapped her arms around his neck. "Those kind of kisses are going to get you in trouble, mister."

"Um, I hope so." He bent down to kiss her lips, ignoring the soapy dishwater dripping from her hands onto his shirt.

Her lips eagerly met his and she tightened her hold on him. His world tilted in the crazy off-course way it did when she kissed him. Or maybe it tilted *on* course. He just knew his world spun dizzyingly whenever she was around him.

She pulled away and laughed softly. "That's not getting the dishes done."

"Don't care about the dishes." He brushed another kiss against her lips.

He heard the racket that always accompanied Josh and Louie's approach and stepped back away from Holly just as the boy and the dog came bounding in the house.

"Hey, are we gonna play croquet again or what? You said we could play one more game after Scotty left."

Holly looked at him and smiled. "I guess we will leave these dishes for later. Duty calls."

He took her hand and they followed Josh outside onto the lawn.

CHAPTER 8

After two days, Steve knew he'd made an excellent decision with hiring Cal. The man was a hard worker and could do the job of two men at once. He was an excellent framer and had done a stellar job tiling the bathroom floor of one of the homes they were building.

Steve walked up to Cal at the end of the second long day of work. "Let's call it quits for today."

Cal looked up and wiped a handkerchief across his brow. "Is it that time already?"

"It is."

"I could do with a cold shower and dinner. I'll pick up Scotty and head back to the Sweet Tea. I need to find a Laundromat in town, too. Scotty and I are sure working our way through changes of clothes in this hot, humid weather."

Steve looked at the man for a minute and decided to

go with his instincts again. "You still looking for a place to rent for a while?"

"I haven't even had a chance to look. I'm going to look this weekend. Can't keep living in the B&B forever, eating all our meals out."

"Well, tell you what. My sister, Lucy, owns the cottage next door to ours. She's rarely home and we rent it out sometimes when she's gone. She won't be back until Thanksgiving this year. Would you like to rent it? I'll give you a break on the rent if you'd be willing to do some painting on it. She's been after me to paint the kitchen, front room, and bedroom. I just haven't found the time. The kitchen is well equipped. Washer and dryer in the laundry room. How about it?"

"That sounds great."

"I'm sure the boys will like having each other next door, too. They seem to have become fast friends. How about you guys move in tomorrow after work?"

"Steve, I can't thank you enough for all your help. The job, the sitter, now a place to rent." Cal reached out a hand.

Steve shook the offered hand. "No problem. Glad I can help out. I know I sure needed help with Josh after his mother left us. I was overwhelmed. Had my momma to help some, but she passed away. Anyway, I know what it's like to need help with raising a boy. Glad to be able to offer some."

"Much obliged." Cal leaned down and picked up his toolbox. "I'm sure Scotty will be thrilled when I tell him. I'll see you in the morning."

"See you." Steve watched the man walk away and

climb into his car. He was glad to help out Cal and Scotty. It wasn't too long ago that he'd been in a similar situation, trying to juggle a job and raise Josh, always worrying he was making the wrong decisions. He reached up and rubbed his shoulder. It had been a long day. He turned to do his quick once over of the job site before heading out to pick up his son.

Cal pushed open the door to the Magnolia Cafe dressed in his last pair of clean jeans and a faded t-shirt. Scotty followed him in with freshly washed hair, clean clothes, and a newly skinned knee compliments of jumping off of a swing today.

Becky Lee looked up from where she was waiting on a customer and waved. He lifted a hand in greeting. Keely showed them to a table by the window. The routine was beginning to feel familiar. It was strange for so many people in town to know him already. He was used to being a loner. Moving around. But already he'd made friends with Becky Lee, Steve and Josh, Rebecca and Larry. Even Keely knew their names and asked about their day.

Becky Lee threaded her way through the tables and came up beside them. "Hi, guys."

"Hi, Miss Tesson." Scotty bounced a bit in his chair and Cal smiled. It was so good to see the boy perking back up.

"How about you call me Miss Becky? That's what my friends' kids call me."

"Okay, I can do that. Right?" The boy looked at Cal.

"Whatever Becky Lee wants is fine with me."

They ordered up dinner and soon were attacking their meals. Cal's stomached rumbled in appreciation like he hadn't eaten in days. He'd been too hot and tired at lunch the last two days to eat much, so he was famished by dinner.

He stealthily—at least he hoped he was stealthy—watched Becky Lee while he ate. She was efficient and friendly with the customers, juggling multiple tables with ease. He needed to do something about the dating angle of their plan. He just hadn't had time to figure that out.

Becky Lee came over with a pitcher of tea and refilled his glass. "You look kind of wiped out."

"Getting used to working in this heat."

"Supposed to break in a few days. Get a bit cooler."

"That'll be nice."

"I hear you're going to rent Lucy's cottage."

Cal looked at her in surprise. "How did you know?"

"Well, Holly came by and she'd talked to Steve."

Cal laughed. "I guess I'm not used to small towns."

"We do know an awful lot about each other's business. Anyway, I was thinking I could drop by tomorrow night. Holly said you were moving in tomorrow? Let me bring groceries for dinner."

"You don't need to do that."

"I want to. I'm off work tomorrow night. It won't be a problem."

It was hard for Cal to keep accepting help from people. It just wasn't something he was used to.

Becky Lee stood waiting for an answer.

She was right anyway. They needed to be seen together. That would help get the town talking it up that they were a couple.

"Sure, that sounds great. We'll see you tomorrow night."

CHAPTER 9

The next morning Becky Lee looked all over her house for her cell phone. She didn't know why it always insisted on hiding from her. She probably shouldn't have gotten her house phone line taken out since the cell phone played hide and seek regularly. She finally found it on the floor of her closet. No clue how it got there.

She slipped the phone into her purse and walked to Bella's house to check on her. Bella had a couple of rough pregnancies with her boys and Becky Lee was worried about her this time. It was a busy season at her shop as well as her recent marriage and her boys trying to adjust to having a stepfather.

She was happy for Bella, she was. But she had to be honest that a pang, deep inside, twitched through her at the thought of Bella having a third child before she, herself, had a chance to even have one. At this rate, she wasn't sure she'd ever have children, and that thought haunted her dreams. She'd always imagined having a passel of kids and a houseful of laughter and love. But she'd never found the right guy to have that with. She'd even thought of adopting a child, maybe an older child, but deep down, ingrained in her soul, was the longing for her own.

But none of that yearning was going to show now. She didn't want Bella to feel awkward and she was truly happy for her friend.

Becky Lee knocked on the door to the carriage house. Normally, she would have just stepped inside, but since Bella had married Owen she'd gotten in the habit of waiting for someone to answer the door. Another change in their lives.

Timmy tugged the door open. "Hi, Miss Becky. Momma's at the kitchen table. Eating crackers. What kind of breakfast is crackers?" The boy slid passed her. "I'm gonna go play outside."

Becky Lee crossed over to the kitchen and sat across from her friend. "Can I do anything for you?"

"No. I'm fine. Just not really up for more than crackers."

"I'm sorry."

"At least it's not sick all day long like it was with the boys. So far, by about ten in the morning, I'm fine. It's just the early mornings." Bella took a nibble of a cracker. "Jenny told me all about Theresa Jean. Oh my gosh. I can't believe it."

"I know. I want to go see her, but Cal says it's not

safe. But… I'm not sure. I think she needs to see—or hear—family. Something to pull her from her coma."

"And you have a nephew."

"Scotty. He's great. I'm trying to get to know him better, though Cal also said it's better if people don't know I'm his aunt. Safer." Becky Lee gathered her hair up and off her neck. It had been a hot walk over to Bella's. "I wish Theresa Jean would wake up and all this hiding could be over. I don't think Cal was exaggerating though. I know his father tried to take Scotty away before. I know Theresa Jean wouldn't want that."

Bella reached across the table and squeezed Becky Lee's hand. "I hope she wakes up soon, too. I'm so sorry all this has happened. And widowed at such a young age. That is so sad. Poor Scotty must be so confused."

"He is. But I think Cal is doing a good job with him. Scotty has been playing with Steve Bergeron's son and that has helped, too. Just having a friend his own age. They are actually going to rent Steve's sister Lucy's cottage."

"That will work out great."

"I think so. I'm going to go over tonight, cook dinner, and stock them up with some groceries. That way I can spend more time with Scotty."

"So what's this Cal like?"

"He's good with Scotty. Patient. He's trying hard. I can see he worries that he's making the wrong decisions." Becky Lee paused for a moment. "I can see the pain in his eyes when he talks about his brother and Theresa Jean. Oh, he calls her TJ. That always startles me a bit. I have a hard time thinking of her as a TJ."

"I bet. I have a hard time thinking of her old enough to have a child. She's still little Theresa Jean to me. Tagging along behind us, always wanting to join in with whatever we were doing."

"And I'd send her home most of the time. I feel badly about that."

"She was ten years younger."

"I should have been more patient with her."

"I remember you taught her to read. And taught her basic cooking. Helped her with homework. You were a great big sister to her."

"Well, I don't feel like one now. How did it get to be so many years without seeing her or hearing from her?" Pain pulsed through her again. Guilt. So much guilt. "I'm going to make it up to her."

Bella's brows furrowed. "She's the one who made the choice to leave. But I hope you two do have the chance to work things out soon."

"Me, too, Izz. Me, too."

Becky Lee loaded up the shopping cart with groceries. Not only for dinner tonight, but staples they would need in the cottage. Bread, butter, milk, coffee, sugar, flour, cereal, boxes of mac and cheese. What did Cal know how to make?

She snagged oranges, grapes, apples, and peaches. Then back an aisle for peanut butter. Then cheese and crackers. She was at a loss on what they liked to eat, and what they would need for lunches. She picked up her favorite tea, then as an afterthought, a six-pack of beer. That would have to do for now.

She hurried home to bake a peach pie for dessert. She had this overwhelming desire to feed the two males. Take care of them. Make sure they didn't go hungry. She shook her head. Surely Cal could cook and feed Scotty.

With a quick glance at her watch, she saw she'd just enough time for a quick shower. She changed into a sundress and sandals. She swore she went through at least two outfits a day with this hot streak of weather.

She loaded up her car and headed over to the cottage. Steve lived on the edge of town on Chalk Road with his sister's cottage right next door. She found the address easily and pulled into the long driveway. Cal's car was already parked in front of the cottage. She glanced over next door and saw Scotty and Josh playing croquet.

Cal came out on the porch and waved. She slipped out of the cool, air-conditioned car and was immediately enveloped in the shimmering late afternoon heat. Cal sauntered across the parched yard and grabbed the bags from her arms. She reached back in the car for two more sacks.

"Looks like you're going to feed an army here." Cal smiled.

"I wanted to get you stocked up for a bit, too." Maybe she had overstepped? She was just trying to help.

"That was nice of you. I appreciate it. I was going to go this weekend and load up."

"Well, this should tide you over."

"I'd say." He grinned and turned to head inside.

She followed him into the small cottage. The front room was decorated simply and comfortably. A large fireplace and hearth graced the back wall. "This is nice."

"It's perfect for Scotty and me. I'm going to do some painting for Steve while I'm here in exchange for lower rent."

Cal led the way into the small, bright kitchen. He set his packages on the counter and reached for hers.

"Let's unpack all this and get it put away in the cabinets, then I'll start some dinner. Thought I'd fry some chicken. Homegrown green beans. Made some potato salad. Peach pie for dessert."

"I could get used to eating like this." Cal grinned and reached inside a bag to begin unpacking the food.

Becky Lee nodded to the last bag. "That one has some cold beer if you'd like one."

"Love one. How about you?"

"Sure. Why not? I do love an ice cold beer on a hot summer night like this."

Thirty minutes later she had the groceries put away, chicken frying on the stove, and green beans simmering with hunks of bacon and onion.

Cal lounged against the counter, his long legs stretched out in front of him, taking occasional sips of beer and keeping her company.

"You should probably go get Scotty and let him get cleaned up for dinner. It will be ready soon."

Cal pushed away from the counter and sauntered to the back door. "We'll be back in a few minutes."

She watched him cross the yard over to Steve's to get Scotty, his tan legs and arms a sign of a man who liked to be outside. He had on worn khaki shorts and a t-shirt that stretched across his broad shoulders. She couldn't help giving him an appreciative stare.

She shook her head. It wasn't like she was really dating him. It was just a pretense so she could see Scotty regularly.

Cal couldn't help thinking how fine Becky Lee looked in her yellow sundress with her hair piled up on top of her head in a careless but adorable way. She'd slipped off her sandals and padded around barefoot in the kitchen. Yes, she was a pretty one. As he walked across to get Scotty, he reminded himself that he and Becky Lee weren't dating. It was all just pretend.

"Come on, Scotty. Time to eat."

"Bye, Josh. See you tomorrow." Scotty dropped his ball and mallet into the croquet set stand and came running over to Cal. He skidded to a stop and turned around. "Bye, Louie."

The dog barked once in answer.

They headed inside and Scotty went to get washed up for the meal. Cal wandered into the kitchen, wanting to help, but knowing he was basically a disaster in the kitchen. He could heat soup. Cook a microwave meal. Make a mean pot of coffee. He was going to have to learn to do better for Scotty. "Can I help you with anything?"

"You could set the table."

That part of 'cooking' he could do. Cal rooted around in the cabinets and drawers and found the plates, glasses, and silverware. He quickly set the table as Becky Lee finished up cooking.

The three of them sat down to eat and an uncomfortable silence fell over the table. Cal shifted in his chair and looked over at Scotty. The boy was enjoying his meal, oblivious to the awkwardness hanging over them.

"Did you have—" Cal started to speak.

"How was your—" Becky Lee spoke at the same time.

They both laughed.

"You first." Cal motioned to Becky Lee with his fork.

"I was just going to ask how your day went. Things working out with Steve?"

"Things are going well. I do like construction work. Making things, creating things, instead of tearing them down. Not exactly what I was raised to do, but I'm glad I've learned the skills. I don't see myself as an office worker anyway. Guess it was a waste of my Harvard education."

"Harvard. That's impressive."

"Yep. Business school, then one year working in my family business before I knew I had to get out of there. It was a cutthroat business and not for me. The family business buys out companies and just… destroys them. Closes them. Incorporates them into our business regardless of the collateral damage. I really hated it."

"So you left?"

"Yes, it was…" How should he put this? "It was an ugly departure. Had to make a clean break. My father basically said to never show my face again."

"I'm sorry." Becky Lee's eyes filled with sympathy.

"Don't be. It was for the best. That kind of life would eat me alive. Eat most people alive. Same reason my brother left."

"But your sister stayed?"

"Let's just say that lifestyle suits her just fine." Cal grabbed another piece of chicken. "Anyway, enough of that. How was your day?"

"I stopped by to see my friend Bella. She's newly pregnant and having a bit of morning sickness. Then I shopped and cooked and got caught up on things around my house."

Cal looked over at Scotty who was just about to fall asleep in his chair. "Hey, kiddo. Why don't you go get ready for bed and I'll come and tuck you in?"

Without any argument at all, Scotty picked up his plate, set it on the counter, and headed down the hallway.

"I think the full day of playing with Josh wore him out." Becky Lee smiled.

"I'm glad to see him having fun. It's been tough on him."

They finished eating and cleared the table. "I'll be back to help with the dishes. Just need to get Scotty tucked in."

Cal went down the hall to Scotty's bedroom. The boy was already in bed. Cal went over and sat on the bed. He saw the familiar look of pain in the boy's eyes. He'd do anything to take away that look. "You okay, kiddo?"

"I miss my mom and dad." Scotty's lip trembled. "It's better when I'm playing with Josh and I'm busy."

"I know it's rough. I'm so sorry. Hopefully, your mom will wake up soon."

"But Dad is gone forever. I miss him." Tears filled Scotty's eyes.

"I do, too, kiddo." Cal leaned over and hugged the boy. "Try to get some sleep."

The boy dashed away his tears. "Night, Uncle Cal. Will you leave that light on?"

"Sure thing, kiddo." Cal left the lamp on and walked to the doorway. He glanced back at the boy curled up in bed. Scotty looked small and vulnerable. The weight of responsibility almost crushed Cal. He couldn't mess this up.

Becky Lee tiptoed down the hallway to the kitchen. She'd gone back to say goodnight to her nephew but had paused when she heard Cal talking to him. She didn't want to interrupt. She'd watched as Cal brushed a lock of hair back from Scotty's face. The lamplight illuminated Cal and she could see the concern etched on his face. For a man who had never taken care of a boy, he was doing a great job with Scotty.

She returned to the kitchen and stood by the kitchen sink, staring out into the night. The poor kid.

So many changes. A few minutes later Cal came into the room.

"Here, let me help."

"You sit down and eat the pie I cut for you. I'm almost finished here. Join you in a sec."

She finished loading the dishwasher and sat down beside Cal.

"This pie is great. Got any more?"

Becky Lee laughed. "Sure do. Help yourself."

Cal got up and cut another generous slice and sat down. "I swear, I'm going to gain ten pounds with your cooking."

Becky Lee doubted he'd gain that weight. His lean, muscled body bespoke a man who could eat huge meals and still stay in shape.

"I wanted to ask you something." Cal put down his fork.

"What's that?"

"Well, Scotty is having a sleepover at Josh's on Friday. That's all right don't you think? To let him sleep over at Josh's?"

"I'm sure it's fine. He'll have a good time."

"I wondered if you wanted to go out while he's gone. I mean, since we're supposed to look like a couple and all. I could take you out to eat. At least that way I could feed you for a change."

"I guess we should be seen out together." Becky Lee fought off the momentary flick of excitement when he asked her out. It wasn't like it was a real date.

"I'll pick you up at six? Where should we go?"

"We could go to Sylvia's Place. It's nice. It's owned

by Bella's husband's brother, Jake, and Jake's mom, Sylvia." She laughed. "Did you follow that?"

"Got it. Sylvia's it is. It's a date." Cal attacked his piece of pie again.

But it really wasn't a date, was it?

CHAPTER 10

Becky Lee flung another dress on the bed in exasperation. Nothing looked right on her. Nothing. She had a pile of skirts and sundresses on the bed. When was the last time she'd gone out on a date? She couldn't even remember. Her dating wardrobe was sadly lacking.

And this technically wasn't really a date.

But, no matter. She needed to find something to wear. Unfortunately, she didn't have time now to go buy something new. She'd gotten hung up at work and only had about fifteen minutes to decide on an outfit and finish getting ready.

She should have called Jenny or Izzy to come help her. They always looked so put together. She swore Jenny could look into a closet and pull out things and put them together in ways Becky Lee would never dream of.

Okay, make a decision. Or you're going to answer the door in your work outfit.

She reached into the back of the closet and found a teal summer dress. Oh, she had red sandals to wear with it, and she'd knitted a lightweight lacy red shawl she could bring in case the air conditioning was chilly at Sylvia's.

Great. A decision was made. She slipped into the dress and sandals and took one look at her hair. No time to curl it now. She quickly pulled it back in a loose French braid. That would have to do. A pair of dangly earrings and she was set.

She stood in front of her full-length mirror and spun around slowly. What did Cal see when he looked at her? A small-town waitress? Did he compare her to Theresa Jean? Theresa Jean was vibrant and funny and the type of person everyone loved.

Okay, so Becky Lee admitted that people liked her, too. But she was more the dependable, steady person with no surprises, no twists or turns in her life. Not much changed in her daily routine. Not that she was complaining, really. She liked her life. Her predictable days. Her familiar routine, her comfortable cottage, a job she enjoyed.

Too much thinking.

She grabbed a bracelet as an afterthought and snatched her purse. She looked around for her cell phone.

Again with the hiding?

This time she found the phone on the kitchen

counter. She really needed to find a spot to place it every single time she came into the house.

A quick knock at the door echoed through the cottage at exactly at six o'clock. Punctual man. She liked that in a person.

She opened the door, and Cal stood in the evening light. He was dressed in khaki slacks and an oxford button-down shirt with the sleeves slightly rolled up. His hair was still damp from a recent shower. The smell of his aftershave wafted across the doorway, a subtle but clean scent.

"You look nice." Cal's eyes shone with appreciation.

She barely kept herself from squirming under his gaze. "Well, thank you. You look nice, too."

"Had to go buy nice clothes. Didn't really pack very carefully when we left town. Bought some more clothes for Scotty, too. That boy gets more dirt on his clothes than anyone I've ever seen. Can hardly keep up with keeping him in clean clothing."

"Boys are like that. Bella says she does laundry every night to keep up with her two boys."

"I'd believe it. Between Scotty's clothes and my work clothes, that washer is running every night for us, too." Cal stepped back a step. "You ready to go?"

"I am. Do you want to walk?"

"I have my car here, but walking sounds nice. There's finally a bit of a breeze tonight."

"We'll walk then." Becky Lee turned, closed the door behind her, and they walked to the sidewalk. "It's just down the street from the cafe on Main Street."

They walked along and Becky Lee pointed out things to Cal as they went. The old elm tree that was struck by lightning last year and part of its bark was singed black. The shop on the corner that finally got a new roof last week after being damaged in the tornado. The city park. The Best Friends' Diner. The vet clinic where Holly worked.

They got to Sylvia's place and walked through the doorway. The restaurant was doing a brisk business. Jake, the owner's son, greeted them at the door. "Hey, Becky Lee. Good to see you here. Two?"

"Yes. Jake, this is Cal. Cal, this is Jake. He and his mother own the restaurant."

Cal reached out and shook Jake's hand. "Nice place."

"My mom's pride and joy." Jake smiled. "Come this way. I have a quiet table in the corner for you."

Becky Lee said hi to a handful of people as they crossed the room. She saw quite a few of them raise their eyebrows as she walked through the room with Cal. She guessed it might have been longer than she thought since she'd had a date.

They stepped outside into the warm evening air. The breeze tickled a few loose locks of her hair. "That was a wonderful meal. Thank you." Becky Lee stepped onto the sidewalk.

"It was. I'm stuffed. Great food. Good wine."

"Well, Becky Lee. Imagine seeing you here."

Becky Lee froze at the sound of Camille's voice. Way to spoil a lovely evening. She turned around with a smile pasted carefully across her face. "Why Camille, nice to see you."

"Who's this handsome man with you?" Camille practically batted her eyes.

"Cal, this is Camille."

"And this is Delbert Hamilton." Camille clutched the arm of the short man standing next to her.

"Nice to meet you two." Cal's deep voice rumbled across the night air.

"Are you two leaving? Delbert and I are just going in to eat. I swear, you townsfolk eat dinner at the most uncivilized early hour. I just do not understand." Camille tossed her curls as she spoke. "Delbert and I never even think about dinner until after eight."

Becky Lee counted to ten, which it seemed like she always had to do around Camille.

"Well, Cal. What brings you to town?" Camille was sizing Cal up and giving Becky Lee a what-did-you-do-to-deserve-him look.

Becky Lee tucked her hand in the crook of Cal's elbow. "He's working for Steve Bergeron."

"Ah. I see." Camille sized up the nicely dressed Cal, obviously reconciling the businessman appearance with her preconceived notion of construction workers.

But then Camille had preconceived ideas about everyone and everything and rarely changed her opinion.

"Becky Lee, I didn't know you even dated anymore.

Good for you for getting a date." Camille's voice dripped with niceness. Fake niceness.

Now what was she supposed to say to that?

Camille didn't notice Becky Lee didn't answer her and continued her litany. "But what a perfectly understated dress. So simple, but then it suits you."

The words understated and simple were said with an undertone that said ugly and out of style.

Becky Lee was determined to not let Camille get under her skin. "Why thank you, Camille. We should let you two go in and have dinner."

Cal was eyeing the two women carefully. With a sudden whoosh of warmth, Cal slipped his arm around her waist and pulled her close. "Yes, you two have a pleasant dinner. So nice to meet you. Becky Lee here is going to show me more of the town, aren't you, hon?"

Becky Lee struggled to keep her eyes from flying wide open. "Um, yes. I am. It's a lovely night for a walk."

Camille arched an eyebrow with the still incredulous look of what-does-he-see-in-you plastered on her perfectly made-up face.

"She's really something." Cal leaned down and pressed a quick kiss on Becky Lee's cheek. She was glad his arm was around her because she would have fallen down in pure surprise. A bolt of lightning shot through her and the world tilted crazily.

Cal continued on in a slow drawl as if nothing had happened. "I'm lucky to have found her."

Becky Lee's pulse was pounding in her ear so that

she could barely hear whatever it was that Camille said as she and Delbert went into Sylvia's. As the door closed behind them, Becky Lee spun around. "What was that?"

"Well, your friend there—who I take it isn't really a friend—I thought she needed a bit of a show. You know, to prove we're a couple."

Becky Lee had to keep herself from reaching up to touch her cheek. It was still tingling and she could feel the heat of a blush.

She steadied her jangled nerves and looked up into Cal's eyes. "I'll tell you one thing, the whole town will know we're a couple by tomorrow. Camille will make sure of that."

"And that was the point, right?" Much to his delight, Cal noticed a rosy blush across Becky Lee's cheek. Guess he'd caught her off guard with that quick kiss. But he hadn't been able to stop himself. He wasn't sure what had come over him. It had seemed like the right thing to do at the time.

"I get the impression you two aren't the best of friends."

"A bigger understatement has never been spoken." Becky Lee sighed. "She's been a thorn in my side since high school days. Putting on airs. The town's biggest gossip. She has a way of getting under my skin. On the surface what she says sounds fine, but underneath it's all little digs. She's self-centered and a troublemaker."

"Tell me how you really feel."

"Okay, I'm not being very kind, but I'm being totally truthful. That guy with her is Delbert Hamilton. I'm surprised you didn't get his full name. Delbert Hamilton of Hamilton Hotels. That's how she usually refers to him, like it's one long name."

"Well, if she's going to spread the word that we're a couple, my job here is done. How about I walk you home?"

Becky Lee's face was covered in a bemused expression and she just nodded. As they headed down the sidewalk, Cal decided it was probably a good idea to take Becky Lee's hand. In the name of making the town think they were dating, that was all it was.

He slipped her small hand into his and she looked up at him for the briefest moment. Some expression flashed across her face, but he couldn't quite figure out what he saw in the depths of those deep blue eyes.

They strolled back to Becky Lee's house, mostly in silence. A few people passed them on the street and Becky Lee said hi to most of them by name. He found it comforting in a way, instead of disconcerting, that everyone seemed to know almost everyone else. He was used to the anonymity of big cities. A small town where a person could feel they belonged and they were a part of it? That feeling was different and yet a bit appealing to him. He'd spent so many years traveling from town to town, job to job. But that's what he liked, right? No strings and the ability to just pick up and go. No one's expectations to live up to. He'd thrived on that the last few years. Thrived on seeing the country, moving every few months, heading out whenever and to wherever he chose.

He turned to Becky Lee. "Do you like living here in Comfort Crossing?"

She wrinkled her brow. "I do. A lot. I grew up here and it's home to me. I don't really have a desire to move somewhere else. I like knowing most of the people. My best friends live here. I just... like it."

"It all seems a bit foreign to me. Like even more foreign than when I traveled the world. Every city I traveled to in the world, I could just get lost in it. I could be anonymous, unnoticed. I imagine that's hard to do here."

"Nigh on impossible to be unnoticed here. Everyone is kind of up in everyone else's business, but usually not in a mean way. Well, except for maybe Camille." Becky Lee laughed.

They reached Becky Lee's house and stepped onto the front porch. She stopped and leaned against the railing. "I was wondering. There's an ice cream social at the town park tomorrow. Do you think Scotty might like to go to that?"

"I'm pretty sure he's never been to a town ice cream social—and neither have I—so I think we should put that on our calendar for tomorrow."

"How about I meet you there about two?" Becky Lee looked up at him.

The moonlight shone down on Becky Lee, illuminating her blonde hair with streaks of magical light. For one brief moment, he wanted to lean down and kiss those lips of hers. But no one was around to give him the excuse. That didn't stop him from wanting to kiss her though.

Things were getting even more complicated.

He cleared his throat and commanded his gaze to move away from her lips. "Yes. Two o'clock. That sounds fine."

CHAPTER 11

Cal looked around the park the next afternoon. Maybe they should have come up with a specific place to meet. The park was crowded with people milling about, kids and adults eating ice cream cones, a group of teenagers playing volleyball, mothers and fathers pushing kids on swings.

It looked like a scene from a romantic movie that guaranteed a happy ending.

But he and Scotty knew better than most that happy endings were never guaranteed.

They walked into the shade under a large live oak. The sun was relentless today.

"Hey look, there's Josh. Can I go play with him?" Scotty danced in front of Cal.

"Okay, but don't leave the park." Cal was unsure, again, if he was making the right decision. Do you let boys run around a park in a small town? Surely it was safe, right? He raked his fingers through his hair in indecision, second guessing himself.

Just then Becky Lee appeared at his side. "Did you get some ice cream yet?" Her smiled dazzled him.

No, it didn't.

"Ah, no. I haven't yet."

Becky Lee tugged on his hand. "Well, let's go get a cone. My favorite is butter pecan. What's yours?"

"I'm a purest. Vanilla. Always."

"Well, you're a strange one Cal Gray, but we'll get you plain vanilla if you insist."

They ate their cones, then wandered over to check on Scotty. He was kicking a soccer ball around with a handful of other boys, covered in streaks of dusty dirt, and having a great time.

"We're going to walk around some more. We'll come back in a bit," Cal called out to Scotty.

The boy grinned, waved, and raced off with Louie barking and chasing after him.

"Next thing you know, he's going to be asking for a dog." Becky Lee laughed.

"Oh, I don't think so. I'm proud that I've managed to keep up with Scotty. To be honest, I don't really keep up with him… it's more like we're surviving. He's a handful."

"Little boys are."

Cal couldn't help but see a wistful look flash across Becky Lee's face, but it was quickly tucked behind a smile.

"Hey, look. There's Camille over across the park. I think she's watching us." Cal tilted his head towards where he spied her. "How about we give her something to talk about?" With that, he leaned down and pressed a kiss against Becky Lee's surprised lips. She startled, then kissed him back tentatively.

Her kissing him back was his undoing. He leaned into her lips, shocked by the feelings coursing through him.

She pulled back suddenly, a shy expression across her face.

"Hm. That was nice." Cal glanced over and saw Camille staring openly at them. "Yep, she saw us."

"Who… what?" Becky Lee stood in front of him with a flustered expression.

"Camille. She saw us kiss."

"Oh. Camille. Right."

Becky Lee couldn't pull a coherent thought out of her head if her life depended on it. What kind of magic did Cal have that totally rendered her senseless? This was all supposed to be a big game of pretend.

That kiss hadn't felt like make- believe to her.

She took a step back and almost tripped. Cal reached out to steady her. Just then Steve and Holly walked up.

"Hi. Thought we saw you two over here. Didn't mean to interrupt…" Steve looked at both of them. "I didn't know you two knew each other."

Holly laughed. "What he's saying, in a not-so-subtle

way, is he saw you kissing. He didn't know you two were dating."

"Yes, um." She looked at Cal for help.

"We've gone out a few times. Becky Lee's been showing me the town. Scotty seems taken with her, too." Cal draped an arm around her shoulder.

A momentary twinge flicked through Becky Lee at the ruse they were playing on the people in the town. But it was all for the good of Scotty. That was what was important.

She glanced up at Cal for a moment and wondered when he'd kiss her again.

No, she didn't.

Yes, she did.

Stop that nonsense.

Great, now she was having whole conversations with herself. She turned her attention to Holly. That would be safe. "So I hear good things about you from everyone who goes to the vet clinic. Do you like practicing here?"

Holly nodded. "I do. I really love it. It's a smaller practice where I can really get to know the people and their pets. I'm just… really happy here."

A big grin spread over Steve's face when Holly said that. Becky Lee hid a smile. It was so obvious the man was head over heels in love with Holly. She wondered if Steve realized it yet. Or Holly. They made a cute couple, and she'd seen how good Holly was with Josh. The boy could use that after his mother left and losing his grandmother.

Steve slipped an arm around Holly's waist. "We're pretty happy she's here, too."

Holly's eyes sparkled and she looked up at Steve.

"Well, we better go. I'll see you Monday morning, Cal."

"Yes. I'll see you then."

Becky Lee watched as Holly and Steve walked away. Steve had his head bent close to Holly's listening to her as they strolled towards the gazebo.

"Do you think someone should tell him that he's in love with Holly?" Becky Lee grinned.

Cal looked at the departing couple. "You don't think he knows?"

"I'm not sure. But if he doesn't, he's the last person in Comfort Crossing to figure it out."

Greta sat on a bench in the shade looking across the park at Becky Lee and some man. She'd seen the man kiss Becky Lee. She was going to have to ask Jenny what was going on there. Jenny hadn't mentioned that Becky Lee was dating anyone.

The sun lit up Becky Lee's hair in the same way it used to set her aunt's hair aglow. Greta remembered being so jealous of Ellie's golden hair. Thick, beautiful, with a hint of natural curl. Becky Lee looked so much like her aunt. Sometimes it was hard to watch Becky Lee and not remember the bittersweet pain of the friendship she'd had with Ellie.

She missed that friendship. She'd had other friends, of course, but none of them had taken Ellie's place. But there was no use in wallowing in self-pity. What was done was done.

Greta sighed. You'd think after all these years, it would be easier to remember those long ago days without it hurting. But sometimes, like today, it seemed like it was only yesterday and the pain was fresh again.

She stood up and brushed some wrinkles from her skirt. It was a scorcher today. So many days in a row of endless heat. Just like that summer so long ago.

But, she wasn't going to think about that anymore. She was going to treat herself to a big cone of chocolate mint ice cream. There wasn't a lot that chocolate mint ice cream couldn't make better.

CHAPTER 12

Becky Lee was glad that Cal and Scotty had plans with Steve and Josh the next day because she had plans of her own. Plans that Cal wouldn't approve of. But no matter what Cal had said, Becky Lee needed to go see Theresa Jean. She needed to talk to her and see if she could get her to wake up. Maybe hearing her voice would bring Theresa Jean around. She had to try.

She was going to be cautious and thought of every possible way she could be careful to the point she felt like she was in some kind of spy movie. Ridiculous, but she did want to protect Scotty, and she was aware that Cal said his father might have people watching Theresa Jean. Or watching Becky Lee for that matter, if he'd looked into Theresa Jean's family.

Becky Lee borrowed Bella's car, saying that hers was having problems. She felt terrible about having to lie to her friend. She'd practically snuck over to Bella's to get the car, with surreptitious looks over her shoulder to make sure she wasn't being followed.

Her heart raced as she sped along the back roads to Baton Rouge in the early morning hours and found the med center where Theresa Jean was being treated. There was no way around it, she was going to have to ask for her room number. Hopefully, that wouldn't be a problem. She couldn't just wander the hospital peeking in rooms.

She asked for the room number at the hospitality desk, but then went to a different floor and wandered around a bit. That's what someone would do in a covert operation, right? She took the stairs back to her sister's floor and walked past her room. A nurse was inside, so she just kept walking.

After she saw the nurse leave, she slipped into her sister's room. The beeping of the machine broke the eerie quiet of the somber room. The room was dark and it took a bit for her eyes to adjust. She wanted to throw open the blinds but didn't want anyone to know she'd been here.

As her eyes adjusted, she stared at her sister, pale and unmoving, hooked up to so many wires. "Ah, Theresa Jean, how did we get to this point?" Becky Lee took her sister's hand. "I've missed you. We shouldn't have let it go on this long without seeing each other. I'm so sorry about your husband. The accident. Everything."

Sorrow seared her, tearing her insides. Guilt over the lost years. Pain at seeing her sister so still in the hospital bed. She choked back tears.

She stared at her sister, willing her to give some sign

that she was hearing her. "It's time to wake up now. Scotty is with Cal and me. He's safe and doing okay. But he misses you a lot. Can you wake up so I can bring you to him?"

Becky Lee squeezed Theresa Jean's hand. "Please wake up." Hot tears roll down her cheeks. She wanted to hurl a pillow at the darn beeping machines. She wanted to scream at the unfairness of it all. But she just stood by her sister's side, willing her strength.

She swallowed the lump in her throat. "I hear you go by TJ now. It kind of suits your personality. I'm going to have a hard time adjusting to calling you that, though. I'll work on it. Cal has a job in Comfort Crossing. I've been helping him with Scotty. Scotty doesn't know I'm his aunt yet. Cal thinks it's safer that way. We're even pretending we're a couple so I have a logical reason for seeing so much of Scotty."

Still no sign of waking up.

"Cal is really great with Scotty. I can tell he really cares about him. He's always afraid he's making a mistake though."

Becky Lee smothered a sob. "I promise I'll keep him safe for you. I will. I swear. But Theresa Jean—I mean TJ—come back to us. We need you. Scotty needs you."

She stared at Theresa Jean's face wondering if possibly there was the slightest wrinkling of her forehead. Was her sister hearing what she said?

Becky Lee startled at a noise behind her and spun around to see a nurse standing in the doorway.

"I was just leaving." Becky Lee squeezed Theresa Jean's hand one more time.

"Are you family?"

"Uh, no. Just a friend."

The nurse came over to check on Theresa Jean and Becky Lee took that as an opportunity to slip away. She would rather that no one had seen her, but she hoped the general comment of just being a friend would cover her visit.

She slipped down the stairs and out the back entrance. She found the car where she'd parked it under a tree for shade to help keep it cool. She climbed into the car, rested her forehead against the steering wheel, and finally allowed the tears to fall freely. The tears turned into ugly sobbing until she was finally spent.

Becky Lee grabbed a tissue from her purse and wiped the tears away. She straightened her shoulders, put on her sunglasses, turned the ignition, and put the car into reverse. Time to take the long way back to Comfort Crossing. She looked around the parking lot, not seeing anyone but a couple with a young child.

Relief washed through her. It looked like she safely made it to see her sister without being spotted by anyone suspicious looking. Now, if only her words registered somewhere in Theresa Jean's brain and her sister started to wake up.

By the next day, Becky Lee was feeling guilty about her trip to visit her sister. Well, not actually guilty about going to see her, but about hiding it from Cal. Surely he'd understand her need to see Theresa Jean. Maybe it had even helped in some way, somewhere deep in Theresa Jean's subconscious.

As if her thoughts could attract consequences, she heard a knock at the front door. She crossed the carpeted floor in bare feet, the worn pile on the carpet reminding her that she'd meant to look for new flooring for the cottage. Most of her to-do list had been put on the back burner since Cal and Scotty had come to town, but she guessed that was to be expected.

She opened the door to see Cal standing on the front porch.

"Hope you don't mind that I just stopped by. I tried calling, but you didn't answer."

Her cell phone. Where was the darn thing?

"No, that's fine." But she self-consciously looked down at her worn shorts and her t-shirt with a big stain on it from painting a side table a few weeks ago. Her hair was falling around her shoulders in a haphazard mess. She reached up and twirled her hair up and slipped another pin in to try to tame it.

"I had to run an errand in town for Steve. Stopped by Magnolia Cafe but they said you weren't working so I took a chance you'd be home. I wanted to ask you over for dinner tonight. Thought you'd like to spend time with Scotty. I'll even cook. That is grill burgers. My only claim to cooking fame."

"I'd love to." Becky Lee figured now was as good a time as any to tell Cal she'd seen Theresa Jean. She looked him in the eye. "I need to talk to you for a minute and don't get mad at me."

"I can't imagine what you could do to make me mad." Cal flashed her an easy smile.

"Well, good." Becky Lee forced herself not to take a step back, squared her shoulders and thrust out her chin in a bit of defiance. "I went to go see Theresa Jean yesterday."

Cal's eyes turned a steely blue and a muscle twitched at his jaw line. "You didn't."

"I had to. I had to see her, talk to her. See if I could get her to wake up."

"I told you how dangerous it was." Cal's voice was a low growl.

"I was careful. Really careful." She stared at his face hoping for signs of understanding.

"I said not to go."

She bristled then, not used to being told what to do. "Well, I went. I needed to see her."

"You've put Scotty in danger."

"I don't think anyone even knew I was there. Just one nurse saw me and I said I was a friend."

"You have no idea what you've done."

"I think it will be okay." Becky Lee was beginning to doubt herself. Cal looked so fiercely protective.

"You have no idea the kind of people you're dealing with." He paused for a moment and cocked his head. "You've never even asked me my brother's name."

Becky Lee wrinkled her brow. No, she hadn't ever asked him. She'd been so wrapped up in worry about Theresa Jean. Cal had always just referred to Theresa Jean's husband as his brother. "What is his name?"

Cal took a deep breath and looked her straight in the eye. "Gordon Scott Grayson."

Cal knew the exact moment when she recognized the name. He could see it in the wide eyes and the way she slowly sagged against the door frame.

"Oh. Those Graysons." Becky Lee looked at him carefully. "Of Grayson Industries. Your brother's arrest was all over the news. Your family is… powerful."

"You mean my family is known as—how do people say it—a crime family?"

"Are they one?" Becky Lee's voice cracked.

"Let's say that my father has many powerful and ruthless friends. And enemies for that matter."

"Cal, I had no idea."

"I was trying to protect you. The less you knew, well I figured you'd be safer." Cal sighed, angry at Becky Lee for going to see TJ, but also angry that by keeping his family's identity a secret, he hadn't impressed on Becky Lee just how dangerous going to see TJ was. He was making so many decisions these days and half of them were backfiring on him.

"I'm sorry." Becky Lee's blue eyes clouded with remorse.

He let out a long breath of air. "Well, what's done is done. If I would have told you the whole truth maybe you wouldn't have gone. You'd have understood the extent of the danger. My father is a powerful man and used to getting his own way. By any means possible."

"I really was careful."

"You need to be even more cautious now. Keep your eyes open. I need to talk to Mrs. Baker and make sure she keeps a close watch on Scotty and explain that even if someone says they are family, not to let Scotty go with them. I've got to keep him safe."

Cal looked at Becky Lee's troubled expression and wondered how the heck he was going to protect not only Scotty, but Becky Lee. For about the millionth time in his life, he cursed his luck for being born into the Grayson family.

CHAPTER 13

After three days of double shifts at Magnolia Cafe and no sign of Cal's father, Becky Lee was beginning to breathe a bit easier. Surely Cal was exaggerating how ruthless his father was. She was actually getting a bit cocky about her covert trip to see Theresa Jean, but not cocky enough to venture another visit. At least not yet.

Becky Lee hung up her waitress apron and called goodbye to Keely. She was headed home for a nice night of sweet tea and knitting on a blanket she'd started for Bella's baby. Just as she slipped out onto the sidewalk she spied Cal approaching with Scotty, Josh, and Louie.

"Hi there. We were just going to see if you wanted to come to the park with us this evening now that it's cooled off a bit." An easy smile played at the corners of Cal's mouth.

"Ya wanna come, Miss Becky?" Scotty looked up at her.

"Sure, I'll come for a while. I was just going to go home and knit for a bit, but some fresh air sounds good."

"Hey, I'll race you." Josh started to run.

"No. Boys. Wait for us." Cal sounded anxious and Scotty skidded to a stop. They crossed the street at the corner and headed into the park. Cal looked around carefully before he seemed to relax a bit.

"I don't want them to get too far away. Mind if we keep moving around close to them?"

"Not at all."

They sat on a bench close to the fort climbing structure. The boys were playing some elaborate made up game of capture the flag.

"They seem to have become fast friends." Becky Lee watched the boys play.

"They have. I figured I'd bring Josh along to the park and give Steve and Holly some alone time this evening."

"That was nice of you."

"Or selfish." Cal grinned. "If Josh is with Scotty, they play and run around and it tires Scotty out. Also, that means I don't have to run around with Scotty after a long day's work." Cal leaned back on the bench, his long legs stretched out in front of him. "He's a hard boy to keep up with."

"I think it's the age. They seem to have boundless energy until they drop."

"That about explains Scotty. I don't know how your sister ever kept up with him when Gordon was in prison…" Cal's voice drifted off. "I guess she'll have to go it alone now, too."

"No, she won't. She'll have me. I'm going to try to persuade her to move here and let me help."

Cal looked across the park and Becky Lee felt him stiffen at her side. He jumped up abruptly and she rose beside him.

"What is it?"

"Trouble."

A man with gray hair and a business suit headed towards them. Cal glanced over at the boys and put his hand on her elbow.

"James." The gray-haired man stood directly in front of them.

James? Who was the man talking to?

"Father."

"James?" Becky Lee couldn't help asking.

"James Calvin Grayson the third," Cal said each word separately as if to punctuate the name.

"Yes, he's my namesake. Even if he didn't live up to the name." The man looked over at her, his gaze sweeping from her head to her toes before dismissing her.

Cal's muscle twitched in his jaw, but he said nothing.

"You're a hard one to find, but I knew you'd mess up eventually. This is the sister, I presume?"

Becky Lee stared at the man. His face was hard with lines etched around his eyes. His haircut was as precise as his pressed trousers. Expensive leather shoes were being covered by the dust in the park. She briefly wondered if he polished his own shoes or had someone who would clean them up for him.

"It was good of you to visit your sister. Made it much easier for me to track down my son."

Becky Lee's heart pounded in her chest. She thought she'd been so careful. Cal was right, she'd made a really big mistake.

The man opened up his suit coat and drew out a folded paper. "I wanted to give this to you personally." He held the paper out to Cal.

Cal stood there not moving.

"Go ahead and take it, son."

Cal flinched but reached out to take the paper. "What is it?"

"It's a motion for a hearing for custody of Scotty. In that ridiculous small town Gordon lived in. Tried to get it moved to Chicago but couldn't do that without putting the whole process back. You know how I like the home court advantage."

Becky Lee's vision swam before her and she stumbled against Cal. He held her steady.

"It's never going to happen. I have legal custody." Cal glanced over at the boys again.

"We'll see about that. We have a hearing set for next week."

"That's not what Gordon wanted and it's not what TJ wants."

"What Gordon wanted doesn't really matter now, does it?"

Becky Lee couldn't believe the coldness in the man's statement.

"Oh, it means a great deal, Father." Cal's voice was laced with cold fury.

"Well, I'll see you in court."

"Don't do this." Cal didn't plead, he just stated it.

"I'm already doing it." The man turned on his dusty leather shoes and stalked across the park.

"Cal, I'm so, so sorry. This is all my fault."

It was Becky Lee's fault, and he was angry at her for not listening to him. Angry at himself for not protecting Scotty better. Angry at his father for trying for custody. Angry at Gordon for dying and leaving him to protect his son.

That last thought punched him in the gut.

What kind of brother was he? He let go of Becky Lee, sank onto the bench, and held his head in his hands.

"I'm sorry," Becky Lee repeated.

He knew she was waiting for him to say it was okay, but it wasn't. It was messed up. He raised his head and looked over at Scotty swinging from the monkey bars off the side of the fort. So carefree. Just doing what little boys do. He'd never get that chance if his father got his way.

"I need a lawyer. Best one we can find. Family lawyer."

"Let me talk to Bella's husband, Owen. He's used a lot of lawyers, maybe he knows a good one."

"I appreciate that. We need one right away."

"I'll call him." Becky Lee dug her cell phone out of her purse and dialed Bella. Cal listened to her side of the conversation while carefully watching the boys. He didn't put anything past his father, like swiping Scotty away. His father always said that possession was nine-tenths of the law. His father had often found sneaky ways to snag majority interest in a company before coming in for the final crushing blow.

Becky Lee sat back down a few minutes later. "John Black. Owen said one of his business partners went through a messy custody battle and this John Black is one of the best in Louisiana. His office is in New Orleans. Owen is calling him now, so he'll be expecting your call."

Cal nodded. "I'll see how quickly I can get in to see him."

"*We* can get in to see him. I'm going with you."

Despite his frustration with her for going to see TJ, he knew she only had TJ and Scotty's best interests at heart. He nodded. "Fine. We'll both go."

Just then his cell phone rang and he dug it out of his pocket. Steve's number scrolled across the caller id. "I better get this."

He listened to Steve. "Just a minute, let me see what I can do." He turned to Becky Lee. "Could you take Scotty back to my place and feed him? And drop Josh off with Holly? She'll be waiting for him at Steve's house. Steve has an emergency at a job site and needs my help."

"Of course, I can. You go on. Scotty and I will get my car and I'll drive him to the cottage. If you're late getting back, I'll put him to bed."

"Thanks." Cal talked to Steve for another minute, promising to meet him at the job site.

He and Becky Lee crossed the park to where Scotty was playing. "Scotty, Becky Lee is going to take you and Josh home. I need to run out to a job site with Steve."

Scotty looked up at Becky Lee. "We're not going to walk are we? Our cottage is far away."

"No, we'll walk to my house and I'll get my car."

"Okay. I'm starving though."

"How about I make you a grilled cheese?"

"That would mean you thought I had bread and cheese at the cottage." Cal let out a long breath of air. *Where had all the oxygen gone?*

"Okay, we'll run by the market first." Becky Lee shook her head.

"And that is why we eat most of our meals out, right kiddo?" Cal ruffled Scotty's hair.

"Right. You're a lousy cook," Scotty said seriously.

"Ouch." Cal clutched at his heart.

"Okay, I'll stock you up on groceries again. Scotty can help me pick out what he likes." Becky Lee turned to Cal. "I've got this. I'll see you later at the cottage."

Becky Lee bought way more groceries than she intended and found out just what Scotty liked and didn't when it came to food. She dropped off Josh with Holly, then she and Scotty went to the cottage and she put the groceries away.

"Want to make your own grilled cheese sandwich?"

Becky Lee turned to Scotty.

"Really? Me?" Scotty hopped from foot to foot. "Yes. I'll know something that Uncle Cal doesn't know how to make."

"He doesn't make grilled cheese?" Becky Lee couldn't fathom not knowing how to grill a cheese sandwich.

"Well, he made grilled cheese one time. It was burnt so bad we threw it away and he opened a can of chicken noodle soup for dinner instead."

"I see. Let's see if we can do better than that."

Becky Lee had Scotty get out two slices of bread, butter one side of each, and grab two slices of cheddar cheese. After teaching him about safety around stoves, no pan handles hanging off the edge, be careful of the hot burners, they proceeded to grill his sandwich.

Scotty carried the plate with his sandwich like it was a priceless treasure and placed it on the table. She gave him a handful of chips and some slices of apple. He finished every bite of his dinner. They worked together on cleaning the skillet, wiping up the counter, stove, and table, and doing the dishes.

"There. All finished." Becky Lee looked around the tidy kitchen. Might as well teach the boy to clean up his cooking mess, along with his cooking lessons. "How about you get your shower and in your pj's. I'll read you a story after that."

"Really? You'll read to me? Mom always did that. Read to me every night."

"Doesn't Cal?"

"No."

"I bet he would if you'd ask him to." Becky Lee

made a mental note to talk to Cal about bedtime stories. "Now run and grab that shower."

Twenty minutes later Scotty was clean, the bathroom was a disaster of towels and dirty clothes, and Scotty had climbed into bed and handed her a book. She'd deal with the bathroom after she read to him. One lesson at a time on cleaning.

She read to him for a while until she could see his eyes starting to droop and a big yawn escaped him. "I think that's enough for tonight. I'll mark our place, so Cal can pick up there tomorrow night if you want him to."

Scotty scooted down beneath the covers. "Leave the light on. I'm not afraid of the dark, but well, I like to be able to see. Thanks for reading."

"You're welcome. Goodnight, Scotty." She so wanted to bend over and kiss him goodnight. To promise him everything would be all right. But she just pulled the cover up over his shoulders.

She took one last look at him as she walked out of the room. She went and tidied the bathroom and put his dirty clothes in the hamper. The hamper that was bulging with dirty clothes. She decided to throw a load of clothes in the washer. As she finished up, she thought she heard a noise. She stood perfectly still, then she knew exactly what she'd heard.

Scotty. Crying.

She walked back down the hallway and entered the boy's room. She sat on the side of the bed and brushed the hair away from his face. She handed him a tissue. "You okay?"

The boy sobbed again. "I miss my mom. I mean Uncle Cal is nice, but I miss Mom. I know Dad is never coming back, but Mom can. If she'd just wake up."

Becky Lee's heart broke into a million pieces. She gathered the boy into her arms and patted his back. His small arms wrapped around her neck as he clung to her. "Oh, Scotty, I'm so sorry. I'm sure your Mom wants to come back to you. I think she needs some more time to get better. I know she loves you very much."

"I know she does. She tells me she loves me to the moon and back times twenty."

Becky Lee was instantly ported back in time. How her own mother had said that to her every night when she tucked her in. She held the boy until his sobs began to subside, stroking his hair and wishing she could do more to take away his pain.

He lay back on the pillow and wiped at his face. "I'm not really a baby like this."

"It's not being a baby to cry about someone you care about and miss." This time, she did lean over and kiss his forehead. "Try to get some sleep. I'll be right down the hall if you need me."

Scotty nodded and slid down under the covers again.

She walked to the doorway and stood for a moment, her heart filled with compassion for all Scotty was going through and how brave he tried to act.

Theresa Jean, you have a really fine son. Becky Lee walked down the dark hallway, brushing away tears of her own.

CHAPTER 14

By late the next afternoon Becky Lee and Cal were sitting in the lawyer's office in New Orleans. Cal had been quiet on the drive over, but Becky Lee didn't really blame him. She knew she'd caused all of this mess. Well, at least her mistake had made it so Cal's father could find him. She couldn't forgive herself, so why should Cal?

The lawyer, John Black, put down his reading glasses after going over the paper Cal had gotten from his father.

"So, the boy's father is deceased and his mother is in a coma?"

"Yes, sir." Cal leaned forward in his chair. "But we're hoping his mother wakes up any time now."

"You have legal guardianship now? Do you have those papers?"

Cal shifted in his chair. "Well, no. I don't actually have the papers. But TJ said she had them drawn up."

"Do you know if they were actually filed in the courts?"

Cal raked his hand through his hair. "Well, no. I'm not certain."

"I'll have my assistant look into it. If they were filed you'll have a stronger case."

Becky Lee swallowed. What if Theresa Jean hadn't filed the papers? What if they couldn't even find the signed papers?

"Now, do you have a steady job?"

"I do. I work construction."

"How long have you had held that job?"

"A week or so?"

The lawyer scribbled on a legal pad. "The job before that. How long did you have it?"

"A couple of months?"

"So, no steady work?"

Cal shifted in his chair. "I move around a lot. I always have a job, but it changes often."

"I see."

"Own a house?"

"No, I'm renting."

"Any children of your own?"

"No."

"Who watches the boy when you're working?"

"I have an arrangement with a sitter."

"What about school?"

"I. Well, it's been summer, so I haven't worried about it."

"Have you at least enrolled him?"

"No, I didn't think of doing that."

The lawyer set his pen down and looked candidly at Cal. "I have to say, your father has a strong case for custody. He has the financial means and stability. I see here that he's already spoken to the headmaster of a private school about enrollment for the boy if he gets custody. He's already raised three children of his own. Your mother will be there for Scotty, too."

"But that's not what my brother or TJ wanted."

"But the court will consider what is in the best interest of the child."

Her heart plummeted. What if Cal's father actually did get custody of Scotty?

"Look, the man is not fit to be a father. I should know."

"To be honest, that's probably going to come across like poor little rich boy sour grapes to the court."

Becky Lee's mind scrambled for a solution. Anything to keep Scotty away from Cal's father. She'd promised her sister that she'd keep Scotty safe. She had to.

"You can't let my father get custody." Cal's voice was low.

"I'll do my best, but the court will see a single man, no steady job, doesn't own a home, never raised a child before."

Becky Lee stood up. "What if he were married?"

"Well, that would help him."

"To someone with a long time job and a home."

"That would help more."

Becky Lee turned to Cal, her heart pounding in her chest. "Marry me."

"What?" Cal sprang to his feet.

"Let's get married. Right away."

The lawyer stood up then. "Tell you what. I'm going to step outside. I don't really think I should hear any more details about this just yet." He picked up his legal pad and pen and crossed to the door. "I'll be back in a few minutes."

The closing of the door echoed through the room.

Cal stared at her, his eyes searching her face. "That's a crazy idea."

"We can be married before next week's court date."

"That's crazy," Cal repeated himself.

"No, it's not. I'd do anything to keep Scotty safe."

"Well, so would I. But marriage?"

"The whole town thinks we're a couple anyway. They'll think it's love at first sight. This could work."

"I don't know." Cal walked over and looked out the window.

She stared at his back, wondering if he thought she was a lunatic and desperate for a man, or if he understood just how much she was willing to do for Scotty and Theresa Jean. "Listen, I'm probably not who or the kind of woman you ever expected to marry. I understand if you say no. I can't blame you if you do turn me down. But I think it's the one way we can maybe save Scotty from being raised by your father."

Cal turned and looked at Becky Lee. She looked a bit uncertain. Like she'd proposed the craziest idea—which it was—and she was sure she was going to be turned down.

He'd always figured he'd never get married. He wasn't really the settle down and get married type. Who would have him? He'd never live up to a woman's expectations of what or who a good husband was supposed to be. He sure as heck had no role model to follow. He'd drifted around for years now, trying to figure out… What was he trying to figure out? What he wanted to be when he grew up? How crazy was it for a man his age to not have figured that out?

Becky Lee was kind and funny. She'd provide stability for Scotty. A home. A steady job. Heck, she'd even cook healthy meals for Scotty.

What the heck did he have to give her in return?

But, to be honest, the idea had merit. It just might be the only way to keep Scotty safe. There were worse things in life than being married to an attractive, fun, caring woman. She wasn't getting a very good deal with him, though. But if they actually did this, they could handle the fall-out of their decision after custody was decided and TJ woke up and got her son back.

But it was crazy… wasn't it?

In a flash of decision, Cal crossed back over to where Becky Lee was standing and took her hand. "Let's do it."

"Are you sure?" Becky Lee eyed him intently.

"I'm sure." Cal squeezed her hand. "Think you can pull off a wedding this weekend?"

"I'll find a way."

"Then it's settled. We'll get married."

The door to the office opened and the lawyer

stepped inside. Cal leaned down and kissed her thoroughly.

∼

Becky Lee's breath caught in her throat and she unconsciously wrapped an arm around his shoulder.

"Want to make it look good for the lawyer," Cal whispered in her ear then winked at her.

Becky Lee sat down, her head spinning. Cal was still talking to the lawyer, but their words no longer registered for her. She was getting married.

Married.

This sure wasn't how she'd dreamed and planned for her wedding, a wedding to the man of her dreams. That was the plan. A long engagement for plenty of time to plan the perfect wedding. And yet, she knew this was the right thing to do. To keep her promise to Theresa Jean. To make up for not finding her sister for all these years. For letting the estrangement go on way too long. She was going to make it up to Theresa Jean. To keep Scotty safe. All of it.

Now, how was she going to pull this off in just days? A simple wedding. She did have a friend who was a wedding officiant. That might work. They had to apply for their license. So much to do.

She wondered if Bella could help her plan the wedding. The woman was the ultimate event planner. Not that it would be an event. Really, it would probably just be she and Cal. Not really anything much to plan except show up and get married. Her thoughts hopscotched from one thing to the next.

It hit her then like a wave knocking her to her knees.

She was going to have to tell Jenny and Bella about the wedding and she wasn't sure how they were going to take the news.

CHAPTER 15

First thing on Monday morning, they applied for their marriage license, then Cal went off to work and Becky Lee went to meet Jenny and Bella at Jenny's house.

Becky Lee pulled up in front of Jenny's new home. It was a cute older two-story farmhouse that the previous owners had added on to so it had plenty of room for Jenny, Clay, and their three kids.

Becky Lee leaned her forehead on the steering wheel. She hadn't thought this all through. Cal and Scotty were going to have to move into her cottage after the wedding. She was going to have to clear out some space. Scotty could have the small back bedroom, but what to do about Cal? There was a small sunroom in the back of the house with a daybed. But what if someone came to the house and saw that Cal lived in the sunroom? What if Scotty talked about Cal not staying in the room with her? Things were just getting more and more complicated.

She pushed open the car door and climbed out, squaring her shoulders, ready to face her friends. She just hoped they would understand.

Jenny opened the door to her knock and gave her a quick hug. "Just in time. I just pulled a cinnamon cake from the oven."

Becky Lee followed her friend to the kitchen. Sunlight poured in through the big picture window in the breakfast nook. Bella looked up from where she sat at the table, leafing through a magazine. "Hey, Bec."

Becky Lee went over to the counter and poured herself some coffee, then sat down beside Bella. "What are you looking at?"

Bella grinned. "A baby magazine. Seems like so much has changed since I had Timmy."

"I can't even imagine how much things have changed since I had Nathan over sixteen years ago." Jenny joined them at the table with a tray of cake. "Help yourself."

Becky Lee took a small china plate with a large piece of cake from the tray. Might as well fortify herself…

"You feeling better, Izzy?" Jenny took a bite of cake.

"I am. Thank goodness. It was only a few days of feeling a bit sick. Now it seems like I want to eat everything in sight. I'm going to look like a whale pretty soon."

"I doubt that." Becky Lee couldn't imagine her petite friend ever looking anything but adorable when she was pregnant. She was one of those glowing pregnant women who never looked awkward or uncomfortable when she was with child.

They chatted, and Bella had a second piece with a shrug of her shoulder and an I-refuse-to-feel-guilty smile.

There was a knock at the kitchen door and Jenny's mother-in-law, Greta, poked her head in. "Oh, hi. I didn't know you all were here."

"Come in." Jenny motioned to Greta. "Sit and have a piece of cake."

Greta joined them at the table. "It's good to see you girls. Don't you love Jenny's new kitchen? So bright and cheerful. I love having them all live next door."

"It is a pretty kitchen." Bella took another bite of her cake. Then another one.

Becky Lee looked over at Greta. Now she was going to have to explain the situation in front of Greta, too. She needed everyone to keep the real reason for the wedding a secret, but she trusted Greta to keep the secret, too.

Becky Lee pushed back slightly from the table. "So I have some news."

"What is it?" Jenny asked.

"Well... I'm getting married Saturday."

Bella dropped her fork. "What are you talking about? To who?"

"Cal Gray." Well, to James Calvin Grayson III, but she still thought of him as Cal Gray.

"But you just started going out with him. I had no idea you'd fallen in love. What's the hurry?" Bella's forehead creased.

"We haven't even met him," Jenny added.

Becky Lee sighed. "It's complicated. Cal's father has filed a motion to get custody of Scotty. He's tried it before and almost got Scotty taken away from Theresa Jean. There is no way she wants Scotty raised by Cal's father."

"What does this have to do with getting married?" Bella asked.

"Everything. See… Cal's name is really James Calvin Grayson III. His brother was Gordon Grayson."

"Grayson. Aren't they supposed to be a… well, crime family?" Greta's brow creased.

"Yes. Those Graysons. And, according to Cal, most of the rumors said about his family are true. He got out of the business, changed his name. So did his brother, eventually. But now his father wants custody of Scotty. Cal said his father is ruthless and Scotty will be sent off to boarding school like he and his siblings were."

"Do you think he has a chance of getting custody from Cal?"

"The lawyer thinks so. He said that Cal is single, hasn't held a steady job, doesn't own a home, just moved to town, hasn't registered Scotty for school yet. I could go on and on with the strikes against him. Plus, he can't find the paper that Theresa Jean said she signed giving him custody. It looks like it wasn't ever filed with the courts, either." Becky Lee looked at her friends with their worried expressions and continued. "So, we decided to get married. We'll have a stronger case to keep Scotty if we're married. I own my home and have worked a steady job forever. Cal is going by the school this afternoon to get Scotty registered for the fall."

"But you can't get married. Not like that." Jenny reached over and touched Becky Lee's arm. "You don't love him, do you? It's just a… marriage of convenience."

"I want to do this. For Theresa Jean. She needs me now to help keep her son safe and I won't let her down."

"But you've always had such dreams for your wedding. It's not even… right… to marry someone you don't love." Bella scrunched up her face. "There has to be a better way."

"Well, I can't think of one and we're running out of time. We need to get married this weekend. Before the court date next week."

"Cal's okay with this crazy idea, too?" Jenny shook her head.

"He is. I'm sure I'm not his dream wife, but he feels like I do about Scotty. We'd do anything to keep him from being raised by Cal's father."

"You can't do this. You just can't." Bella stood up and paced the floor.

"I am doing it. I'd love your support, but if you can't give it to me… well, I'm still getting married on Saturday."

"Sometimes a person has to make really hard decisions to protect someone." Greta looked over at Jenny. Jenny sighed because she knew ever so well the lengths she'd gone to keep her son Nathan's father a secret. And she hadn't been in love with Joseph when she married him to help hide her secret. How could she argue with Becky Lee, when she was just trying to protect a child, too?

"If this is something you think you have to do, then I'm one hundred percent behind you. Just be sure, Bec." Jenny got up and gave her friend a hug.

"I am sure. I want to do this."

"But all your dreams about getting married." Bella still paced back and forth.

"I'm okay with this, really."

"But if Theresa Jean wakes up, she'll get custody back and then what?" Bella slipped back into her chair.

"We'll figure it out then. But for now, this is what we need to do. And it needs to look legitimate to everyone. Cal's father will be looking at us closely, I'm sure. So the reasons need to be kept a secret."

"Of course, dear." Greta nodded.

Bella let out a long, drawn-out sigh. "Well, if you're sure, then a wedding on Saturday it is. Where are you going to get married?"

"I'm not sure. Maybe at the cottage. I'm going to ask Luke Zuckerman if he'll marry us. I heard he's a marriage officiant now."

"We are going to make this a real wedding. That much is for sure. I'm going to take over planning it. We'll have it at the carriage house, I still have the arbor there from Jenny and my weddings. We can get a cake from Sylvia's." Bella jumped up and grabbed a notebook from her purse. "We'll need to find you a dress."

"How about the dress I wore in my wedding? The

vintage one Izzy found?" Jenny thought that with a bit of alteration the dress would fit Becky Lee.

"That would be nice to be married in the same dress you wore."

"Hey, that could be your something borrowed." Bella jotted some more notes. "I'll order your bouquet. It will be beautiful, I promise."

"You guys don't need to go to a lot of fuss."

"Nonsense. If you're going to have a wedding, it's going to be a nice one. Besides, you said you wanted it to look legitimate." Bella tapped her pencil.

"Bec, there is no way to stop Izzy when she gets her mind made up about planning something. I'd just let her run with it." Jenny smiled. Bella was at her best when planning an event. She thrived on it.

"I'll be glad to help you girls in any way I can," Greta offered.

"All right then. We have a busy week. Let's get started." Bella dug out her cell phone. "I have calls to make."

Jenny looked over at Becky Lee. Her friend looked a bit overwhelmed. One thing was certain, if Becky Lee needed to do this, to marry Cal, they were darn well going to make sure she had a nice wedding.

Greta left the girls to work out plans for Becky Lee's wedding. She took the pathway between her house and Jenny's. The walk was less than a mile and wove among a grove of trees. Clay had put in a gate in the fence between their properties and cleared the pathway. She often walked over to visit, or the kids would come over to her house after school for snacks.

She walked along thinking about Becky Lee and her reason for marrying Cal. She, better than most people, knew that sometimes people got married for all sorts of reasons.

Like Ellie and Martin.

A pang of hurt jangled her nerves, a pain she hadn't let reach her in a long time.

As she crossed into her yard, she looked over at the swing in the live oak tree. That's where Martin had told her. Right there. So many, many years ago.

Where he'd told her that he was in love with her.

She still remembered every detail. The way her heart had fluttered in her chest and her breath had caught in her lungs. The way his lips had felt when he leaned down to kiss her.

Then he'd taken her hand and told her that even though he loved her, he had to go away with Ellie. He was going to marry Ellie. It was the right thing to do.

Yes, she remembered every detail of the day her world had been turned upside down.

CHAPTER 16

Becky Lee hurried down Main Street. She'd spent fifteen minutes looking for her cell phone before she found it, and now she was late meeting Cal and Scotty at the park. She looked down the street and saw Camille. She quickly glanced to the side, wondering if she could make a quick detour down the side street.

Camille waved to her. Her wave looked like she was waving to a crowd from her throne on a beauty pageant float.

Doggone it. Too late to duck away.

Becky Lee pasted a smile on her face and continued toward Camille.

"Oh, Becky Lee. I just heard the news. You're getting married."

"I am."

"Well, the funniest thing happened this week." Camille's voice held a fake conspiratorial tone. "Delbert ran into Mr. Grayson of Grayson Enterprises right here in Comfort Crossing, of all places. Mr. Grayson said he was visiting his son. Delbert mentioned he didn't know a Grayson in town, and Mr. Grayson said his son goes by the last name Gray."

Camille reached out and touched Becky Lee's arm. Becky Lee tried to keep herself from jerking her arm away.

"That wouldn't be your Cal Gray would it? You're marrying a *Grayson*?" Camille's eyes were wide with disbelief and a not-so-subtle look of he's-too-good-for-you.

"He has nothing to do with Grayson Enterprises." Not that it was any of Camille's business.

Camille continued as if she hadn't even heard Becky Lee. "You know, the Graysons are a *powerful* family. Lucky you, he's quite the catch."

"As I said, Cal has nothing to do with his family."

"Well, of course, he does. He can change his last name, but he's still a Grayson." Camille spoke to Becky Lee as if she were explaining something to a toddler.

"I've gotta run. Thanks for the good wishes." Becky Lee was very aware the Camille hadn't offered best wishes or anything remotely close to it.

"I hope Delbert and I get an invite."

"Oh, it's just going to be family." Not that she would invite Camille to her wedding if she were having a two hundred person wedding.

Becky Lee turned and hurried away.

"See you soon," Camille called out.

Not if I see you first.

Cal looked around the park for Becky Lee. She'd promised to meet him and Scotty here. They were going to tell Scotty about the wedding. Cal paced nervously back and forth, watching Scotty play in the fort, while keeping an eye out for Becky Lee.

He finally spotted her coming down the walkway and waved. He watched her carefully as she approached. She was dressed in a simple sundress which seemed to be her preferred outfit on these hot summer days when she wasn't working. This dress was a pale teal color and she'd piled her hair up in the messy way he thought looked so good on her.

He was going to marry this woman.

Doubts and nervousness welled up. Why would someone as pretty and smart as Becky Lee even consider marrying him?

He knew why. Normally a woman like Becky Lee wouldn't have taken a second look at him. Well, back when he was a Grayson, he had beautiful women who wanted him... but it was all about his money. Once he no longer had that Grayson name and money, he'd lost a lot of his allure. Plus, it was kind of hard to have a relationship when he moved around all the time.

"Hi." Becky Lee looked up at him with a nervous smile on her face. "So are we ready to do this?"

"I guess so. Yes." He looked over and saw Scotty watching them. He quickly wrapped one arm around Becky Lee and bent down and kissed her on the lips.

The deliciously soft lips.

She offered a little gasp but kissed him back tentatively.

Cal pulled his lips off hers and leaned close to her ear. "Scotty is watching."

"Oh." Becky Lee's face was covered in the most adorable blush.

He kind of liked making her blush and catching her off guard.

Cal turned and waved at Scotty to come over. The boy came running, skidded to a stop in front of them, and eyed them both suspiciously.

"We've got something to tell you, kiddo."

"What's that?" Scotty looked from Cal to Becky Lee.

"Um. Well, we're getting married." Cal watched closely for Scotty's reaction.

"Who is?" Scotty's eyes narrowed.

"Becky Lee and I."

"Really?" The boy cocked his head, eyeing them both.

"Yes, this Saturday." Becky Lee's voice came out with a bit of a croak when she said the word Saturday.

Heck, he couldn't blame her. It was a lot to process.

"Yes, this weekend. Isn't that great?" Cal looked at the boy, still hoping for a positive response.

"Well, that's cool. Miss Becky is fun and she cooks a lot better than you do. Can I go play again?"

Cal laughed out loud. "Yes, you can go play."

Scotty started racing away then paused. "Hey, I don't have to wear a tie or anything to the wedding do I?"

"Not if you don't want to," Becky Lee assured him.

The boy continued his run to the fort to join a handful of other boys.

Cal shook his head. "Well, that was easier than I thought."

"Hey, I can cook better than you. What more does a boy want?" Becky Lee teased him.

"Now I guess we can move on to the planning the wedding stage."

"I've got that all covered. Saturday at my friend Bella's place. Simple. Just a few people. I called my friend Luke, and he'll officiate. Jenny and Bella are mentioning around town here and there about the wedding. Saying it's just family. Soon the whole town will know."

"What can I do to help?" Cal marveled at all Becky Lee had already arranged. "Oh, what should I wear? How fancy is this going to be?"

"Not fancy. I'm borrowing Jenny's vintage dress. You can just wear slacks and a dress shirt."

"You sure you're okay with all of this?" Cal looked closely at Becky Lee. "I know women dream about their wedding… and this is… well, I'm sure this is nothing that you ever dreamed of."

"I am sure. It's fine. I am a bit uncertain of the whole until death do us part type of vows, though. All the traditional things people promise."

Cal nodded. How could they pledge all those things and not mean them?

"And not to make things more complicated than they already are, but I guess you two will be moving in with me? I have a bedroom for Scotty, no problem. I need to clear out a bunch of yarn and knitting stuff. It's my yarn stash room right now. There's an extra bathroom in the hallway. But... well, what do we do about you?"

Cal wanted to slap his forehead with a duh moment. Of course, they needed to figure out sleeping arrangements.

"I do have a sunroom with a daybed, but what happens if someone comes over and sees that you live back there? Or what if Scotty lets slip that your bedroom is the sunroom?"

Cal frowned. "I... just don't know."

"I guess I could clear out part of my closet and you could put your things in there. Wait until after Scotty goes to sleep to head to the sunroom?"

"That will have to work. I'll make sure I'm up before Scotty. He'll never know. I can share the hall bathroom with Scotty. I'll tell him yours is full of women stuff and it's easier to use a guy bathroom." Cal grinned. "I assume that part is true?"

Becky Lee laughed. "That part is true. I have taken over every available inch in my bathroom."

"Well, that takes care of the living arrangements. Scotty and I will move in after the wedding."

"Good."

"Next week after things settle down, I'd like to take a trip to Baton Rouge. Get more of Scotty and my things. Look around TJ's home and see if I can find that missing paper giving me custody."

"I don't feel like things are ever going to settle down, but let's do go to Baton Rouge. I want to see Theresa

Jean again. We'll do that and get things from her home for Scotty."

"Sounds like a plan."

"I better head out. I have a ton of things to do."

"I'll talk to you tomorrow. Make sure to tell me if there is anything I can do to help."

"I will." Becky Lee headed back down the walkway and he watched as she disappeared around the corner.

He turned back to watch Scotty play, feeling a little lost and not liking the feeling. How in the world was all this going to work out?

After Cal put Scotty to bed, he sat at the kitchen table with a pad of paper and pencil. There was one thing he could do. He could write vows that he and Becky Lee could promise. Things they could promise each other that wouldn't be lies.

He could do this.

He scratched away at some ideas and crossed off just as many ideas as he came up with. He got up and went to the fridge to grab a beer. He took a long swallow of the cold liquid and sighed. This was going to be harder than he thought.

He determinedly crossed over to the table and sat back down. He could do this. He could.

He started to write:

I take you as you are, unconditionally, to be by your side...

CHAPTER 17

Bella glanced at her notebook to make sure everything was going as planned. The arbor had been decorated with mini-lights and ivy. A handful of chairs had been placed in the yard. Becky Lee hadn't wanted to walk up an aisle, so they were all just going to gather at four in the afternoon.

Luckily the heat wave had broken. It would still be hot, but not smothering hot. She'd also put a few fans outside blowing on the arbor and the chairs.

Jenny was picking up the bouquet and bringing it over with her. Becky Lee should be here any minute. Owen had picked up the wedding cake, and it was sitting on the table she'd decorated with flowers. They'd have a small reception inside her home after the ceremony.

She turned at the sound of a knock at the door. "Come in."

Becky Lee walked through the door. Bella took one look at her and hurried over. "What's the matter?"

Becky Lee forced a weak smile. "Nothing? I mean, I'm getting married today. Why would I be feeling shaky?"

"Oh, hon. It's going to be okay. Really." Bella hugged her friend. "Though there is still time to change your mind."

"Not going to happen."

"Then let's go back in my bedroom and get you dressed and ready. I'm going to do your hair. I have flowers I'm going to tuck into it. You'll look great."

Bella led her friend to the bedroom and helped her get dressed in Jenny's wedding dress. It looked spectacular on her.

"Look, I bought you these heels to wear. See, aren't they adorable? Teal toes on them. Your favorite color."

"I love them." Becky Lee took the shoes out of the box. "They're perfect."

"I thought so. I know you love teal—which is really a kind of blue—so now you have your something borrowed and something blue. The dress is vintage, so it's your something old, the shoes are new, so you're all covered."

Becky Lee laughed. "I guess you do have it all sorted out for me."

"Now, sit down and let me do your hair. I'm going to do it up with a few curls hanging down. And just a few sprigs of flowers."

"I'm at your mercy." Becky Lee slipped into the chair in front of the mirror.

Jenny came into the bedroom when Bella was finishing. "It looks great." Jenny came and stood beside the mirror. "Oh, and I put the bouquet in the fridge."

"Thanks." Bella tucked one last sprig in Becky Lee's hair. "There, what do you think?"

"I think you need to come do my hair all the time." Becky Lee smiled.

Becky Lee stood up and walked over to a full-length mirror in the corner. She turned this way and that. She really did look like a bride. She even felt like a bride. Nervous. Excited.

You are a bride, silly.

"You two did so much in so little time. I can't begin to thank you enough."

"Of course, we helped you. Wouldn't have it any other way. If you're going to get married, you're going to have a beautiful wedding." Bella stood behind her, smiling.

"You do look beautiful, Bec." Jenny came and stood beside her, too.

She probably was the luckiest woman in the world to have these two friends. They were always there for her. Always supported her. She didn't know what she would do without them.

"You guys know I love you, right?" Becky Lee fought back tears.

"We love you, too." Bella squeezed Becky Lee's arm. "I'm going to pop outside and see if everyone is here."

"Okay, thanks." Becky Lee hadn't invited many people. Jenny, Clay, and Greta. Bella and Owen, of course. Cal had wanted Steve and Holly to come, so they invited Josh, too. Scotty had been pleased about that. She'd invited Keely since she'd worked for her forever, and her boyfriend Hunt. She didn't think the town would believe there was an actual wedding without at least a few others besides Jenny and Bella.

Bella came back in after a few minutes. "Everyone is here. I had them all sit down. If you want to come outside now, we'll get started." She handed Becky Lee the bouquet.

Becky Lee took one last look in the mirror. One last look at herself as a single woman. She would be a married woman the next time she looked in a mirror.

A married woman.

She took a deep breath. "All right. I'm ready." She actually thought she might be ready. Everything was going to be okay. *It was. Wasn't it?*

Cal stood by the arbor shifting his weight from foot to foot. When he realized he was clenching his fist, he forced himself to relax. *It was going to be okay. Wasn't it?*

He looked up and saw Jenny and Bella come outside. Then he saw Becky Lee. She looked... stunning. To be honest, she took his breath away.

This beautiful woman was going to marry him?

She came up beside him and smiled at him. Her smile gave him strength.

"You look beautiful."

Becky Lee blushed. "Thank you."

"Really beautiful."

"I… uh… are we ready to start?"

Luke stood in front of them. "I think we are ready." Luke thanked everyone for coming then looked at Cal. "Cal here wrote the vows."

Becky Lee looked up at him then, her eyes wide with surprise and appreciation.

He leaned close and whispered in her ear. "Hope that's okay."

She nodded.

"But I'm going to read them because I was too nervous to memorize them."

The paper shook in his hand a bit as he started reading. "I take you as you are, unconditionally, to be by your side. I vow to respect you, encourage you, and care for you. I will share my life with you, all of life's adversities and triumphs. I vow to work with you to build a life together, better than we could imagine. To share adventures and laughter. To be there for you as your spouse and friend."

He looked at Becky Lee and saw tears in her eyes. At that moment, he wanted all those things he'd just promised her… and more.

"Those were beautiful." She leaned up and whispered to him.

Becky Lee reached for the paper and read the vows back to him, her voice broke in the middle and she took a second to collect herself before she finished saying the vows.

"Now the rings." Luke looked at them.

"Oh, I didn't…" Becky Lee looked worried.

"Got us covered. Jenny helped me pick out yours." Cal assured her.

Luke took the rings from Cal. "Repeat after me. With this ring, I thee wed."

Cal repeated the words and slipped a simple silver wedding band on Becky Lee's finger.

Becky Lee smiled at him and squeezed his hand.

"Now, Becky Lee." Luke handed her Cal's ring.

"With this ring, I thee wed." Becky Lee slipped the ring on his finger and he stared at it for a moment. He'd never worn a ring of any kind. Ever. The simple silver band looked out of place on his roughened hand.

Luke cleared his throat. "With the power vested in me by the State of Mississippi, I now pronounce you united in marriage. I give you Cal and Becky Lee."

Cal leaned down and kissed Becky Lee, lingering longer than he probably needed to, but not as long as he wanted to. He took her hand in his and they walked out to greet their guests.

Becky Lee sipped a glass of Champagne as she stood with Jenny and Bella, not really listening to their chatter. She was watching Cal across the room, talking to Steve and Clay. He seemed relaxed now that the ceremony was over.

She looked him over slowly, from his hair in slight need of a haircut, to his clean-shaven face, to his teal dress shirt—had Bella or Jenny told him that teal was her favorite color? His slacks were neatly pressed and he had on freshly polished loafers. He was a handsome man. Very handsome. When he smiled at something the men said, his mouth quirked up in a charming way.

His rough hands were wrapped around a glass of tea. Every so often she'd see him look around for Scotty, to make sure he was okay, then turn his attention back to the men.

"Bec, have you heard a word I said?" Bella stood staring at her.

"What? Well, not really. I'm sorry. I'm kind of lost in my own world right now."

"I was just saying that we got you and Cal a cottage on the beach near Bay St. Louis to stay tonight. A honeymoon. Kind of."

"What? We don't need a honeymoon. And there's Scotty."

"If nothing else, you going away for a night will make the wedding more legit. Plus, I think you could use the break. It's not a long drive. And we already talked to Steve. He's going to keep Scotty tonight." Jenny pinned her with a don't-argue-with-me look. "And we packed a picnic dinner to take with you."

"I don't know…"

Greta came walking up to them. "What don't you know about?"

"They planned us a… honeymoon." Becky Lee shook her head.

"Well, I think that's a splendid idea. Do you good to get away for a bit." Greta smiled. "I'm proud of you girls for being so supportive of Becky Lee. She needed it. She was doing what she thought she needed to do. Friends should support their friends' decisions."

"We couldn't let her get married without a nice wedding. That would be just wrong." Bella looked appalled at the very idea of not throwing her friend a lovely wedding. "Besides, this marriage is what Becky Lee wants. We're behind her all the way… it just took me a few minutes to get used to the idea."

"I still don't know about this honeymoon…" Becky Lee glanced over at Cal.

"Well, we do. I'm going to go tell Cal, then we're going to give you two a send-off." Jenny turned and walked over towards Cal.

"I was going to help take things down and clean up." Becky Lee looked around at the mess in Bella's house, not to mention the chairs and decorations outside.

"Not a chance." Bella shook her head. "You're the bride."

Becky Lee watched as Jenny told Cal. He actually smiled at her and thanked her. Maybe he thought it was a good idea? Well, it would look good if people thought they had a honeymoon night. That was all it was. Another check mark for their scheme.

But with that thought, a wave of sadness drifted over her. All this fuss for the wedding. She was married.

Married.

To a nice guy. A handsome guy. And Cal would have a better chance of keeping Scotty.

Greta walked up and hugged her.

Cal crossed the room and her heart beat faster the closer he got to her.

"I hear we have a honeymoon to attend." Cal winked at her.

"I guess we do."

"Here are the directions." Bella handed her a piece of paper. "Why don't you guys run by your places and grab an overnight bag and head out? Tomorrow when you get back, you can get Cal and Scotty settled into your cottage."

"Thanks for everything, Bella. The wedding was wonderful. It was kind of you to have it here." Cal smiled at Bella.

"I was glad to do it. Now you two run along. You can get to the beach before nightfall and take a walk. I know Becky Lee loves her beach walks."

Becky Lee hugged Bella and whispered in her ear. "You're the best."

Jenny came walking over. "Here's the picnic dinner. Can't have you two starving."

Cal reached for the basket and warmth from his other hand spread through her arm where he had taken her elbow. He led her out of the house into the early evening sunlight.

"A honeymoon. Well, I never." Cal grinned.

They did get to their beach cottage before sunset. Cal carried in their overnight bags and Becky Lee carried in the picnic basket.

"Well, it's a cute cottage." Becky Lee walked through checking it out and admiring the beachy decor. "Two bedrooms. I'll set the picnic basket in the kitchen."

Cal put the bags in the separate bedrooms. Becky Lee noticed he gave her what she would consider the master bedroom. He really was a considerate man.

Becky Lee opened the basket. "We have a six of beer, a bottle of wine, sandwiches, fruit, and some slices of pie."

"Quite a feast. Did Bella make it?"

Becky Lee laughed. "No, I doubt it. Izzy has her strong suits, but cooking isn't one of them. It looks like food from Magnolia Cafe. I'll throw the beer in the fridge, though they had it packed in ice. Do you want to take a walk on the beach?"

"That sounds good." Cal waited for Becky Lee to put the beer and fruit in the small fridge.

They headed out the door and across the road to the beach. Becky Lee kicked off her shoes and stepped onto the warm sand. The heat of the day was behind them, and the sky was beginning to turn a brilliant orange-pink.

Cal slipped off his shoes and fell into step beside her. They walked along the water's edge. The water gently lapped the shore, more lake-like than ocean. A blue heron stood on the shoreline. Becky Lee paused to watch the majestic bird and its antics. The bird stretched its wings, hopped along the shore a bit, then with a whoosh of its large wingspan, it swooped up into the air.

"A blue heron." Becky Lee nodded toward the bird flying away into the distance.

Cal put a hand up to shade the rays of sun from his eyes and looked in the direction of the giant bird. "They really are magnificent birds, aren't they?"

She couldn't agree with him more. They continued along the beach as the sunset grew more brilliant with each passing minute.

"That's some sunset." Cal paused and stared in the direction of the setting sun. "Honestly, maybe I don't take the time to look at many sunsets, but that has to be one of the most beautiful ones I've ever seen."

Becky Lee had to agree with him on that, too, and she was a person who always did look up to check the sunset. "It's beautiful."

They stood in silence, side by side, as the sun slid below the horizon and the sky burst into flames. It seemed sacrilegious to talk in the presence of such splendor.

The sky darkened and a few stars began to blink in the distance. "I guess we should head back to the cottage."

Cal nodded. He reached over and took her hand and tucked it in the crook of his elbow. It surprised her, and yet it didn't. They'd connected somehow, standing there in the remarkable miracle of nature and its brilliant sunset.

Cal held open the cottage door for Becky Lee to go inside. She brushed the sand from her feet and stepped in. He did the same but left the door open with just the screen door closed. The night had cooled and the humidity dropped. A cool breeze blew in from the ocean.

"Let me set out dinner." Becky Lee headed toward the kitchen.

"I'll help." Cal trailed after her, content and relaxed.

They ate their picnic supper, then went out to sit on the wide front porch, choosing the comfortable swing hanging in the corner. Cal took a beer with him, and Becky Lee had a glass of wine.

Cal lazily pushed back a bit, letting the swing sway back and forth.

"It was a nice day, wasn't it?" Becky Lee looked at him.

"It was. Your friends did a great job with the wedding."

"And I'll be forever grateful to you for writing those vows. They were vows I could say and mean them."

Cal was pleased that Becky Lee liked the vows he'd written. He'd been a bit unsure, but he'd known she didn't want the traditional vows. Not with their wedding arrangement. They couldn't vow to love one another until death.

For the very briefest moment he was sad that they hadn't been able to have those vows. He wondered what it would be like to marry someone who he was so in love with that he wanted to spend the rest of his life with her.

That reminded him, he'd almost forgotten. "I'll be right back." He hurried inside and dug a small wrapped present from his bag. He went back out and sat beside Becky Lee.

"I got a little something for you."

"What? Oh, I didn't even think to get you a wedding present." Becky Lee looked embarrassed.

"You didn't need to. I just thought… you might like this." He handed her the present.

She carefully unwrapped the box and opened it. "Oh, a watch."

"Not just any watch… it talks to your cell phone. If your phone rings, the watch vibrates on your wrist. You can also use it to make your cell phone ring if you've misplaced it…"

Becky Lee laughed. "I see you've already got me figured out. Constantly losing the darn phone."

"Well, I figured with things the way they are, and you watching Scotty and all, it would be good to see if we can keep you in better contact."

"I love it." She flashed that dazzling smile of hers at him. "You're a thoughtful gift giver. You'll have to help me get it to talk to my phone. I'm not that techie about things like this."

"I'll set it up for you and show you how it works. You can read text messages on it. Send them from it."

"I feel like some kind of futuristic spy. This is great. I still feel badly that I didn't get you anything."

"Don't. I just thought this might make things a bit easier for you."

They sat contentedly on the swing, gently swaying in companionable silence. He looked over at Becky Lee, lost in her own thoughts and staring into her wine glass. He was fine with marrying this woman. He was. She was amazing. Strong in her convictions. Caring.

And beautiful.

So beautiful that he wanted to lean over and tuck the wayward curl that had escaped the pulled up hair while they'd walked along the beach.

At that very moment, he wished there was someone around to give him a reason to kiss those lips of hers.

She looked up suddenly as if she had felt his thoughts. "You okay?"

His ears burned and he cleared his throat. "I'm okay. Just thinking about today."

"Me, too."

"Are you sorry you married me?" Cal's insecurities raced through him.

"No, I'm not sorry. I'm not sorry at all." Becky Lee smiled a wistful smile. "It was a lovely day."

Cal pushed with his foot again, and the swing creaked as it started back in motion. "It was a good day."

CHAPTER 18

Becky Lee stood in the middle of her front room while Steve and Cal carried in Cal and Scotty's things, some left-over food from their place, a few suitcases and duffle bags. Not a lot of things, but still, it was hard to squeeze anything else into her small cottage.

Scotty and Josh checked out his new bedroom, then raced outside to the backyard to kick a soccer ball around.

"Thanks for watching Scotty last night." Becky Lee started unpacking some boxes in the kitchen while Cal and Steve grabbed some beers from the fridge.

"My pleasure. The boys ran hard until bedtime then dropped like rocks. Works for me."

"Do you want a beer?" Cal held up an ice cold beer towards her.

It looked good. Really good. She should get her kitchen organized though and get the food put away.

But the beer looked really good. But the boxes... "Sure, I'll have one."

Cal grinned and popped the top on a bottle and handed it to her. "You need a glass?"

"No, I'm a bottle drinker."

Steve grinned. "Good for you."

The three of them went out to the back patio and sat in the shade of the towering pine tree.

"Not much of a honeymoon for you two." Steve leaned back in his chair.

Becky Lee almost choked on her beer until she realized Steve was talking about the honeymoon only being one night—not about what did or didn't happen on the honeymoon.

Cal winked at her when Steve wasn't looking.

She shifted in her seat and raised her eyebrows back at him.

"So you said you'd be back to work on Tuesday?" Steve interrupted their silent conversation.

"Yes, we're going to head to Baton Rouge to pick up more of Scotty's things and more of my stuff. Not that I have much more."

Becky Lee wasn't sure where they were going to put what Cal had already brought, much less where they'd put even more of their belongings.

Steve took one more long swig of beer and put down the empty bottle.

How did men drink a bottle of beer so quickly?

"Come on, Josh. Time to go. Let's let these three get all settled in." Steve turned to Cal. "You're still leaving

Scotty with Mrs. Baker tomorrow while you go to Baton Rouge, right?"

"Right. I'll drop him off first thing in the morning."

"Okay. Have a safe trip and I'll see you on Tuesday."

Josh and Scotty came racing up and skidded to a stop before bumping into Steve.

She'd like to have about a tenth of their energy. Becky Lee pushed out of her chair. "Here, I'll walk you out."

She led them to the front door and waved as they left. Scotty settled down in the front room, kneeling by the coffee table, and started working on another jigsaw puzzle she'd left out for him.

She slowly walked through the house, ignoring boxes and suitcases, and headed back outside to finish her beer. Time enough to get it all sorted later.

But it was very unlike her not to sort first, relax later. Is this what marriage had done to her?

A little later, Cal helped Becky Lee put things away in the kitchen. They unpacked Scotty's things and put them in the closet in the back bedroom, the closet he shared with Becky Lee's yarn stash. Becky Lee made a light dinner and it had the expected effect on a hard-playing seven-year-old, and Scotty quickly crashed on the sofa.

Becky Lee watched as Cal carefully scooped up Scotty and carried him to bed. She followed them back to the boy's bedroom and leaned against the doorway as Cal put Scotty to bed. She stood mesmerized by how efficiently he got the boy ready for bed. Gently. Calmly. How had he gotten so competent so quickly? He pulled off Scotty's shoes and helped the almost sleeping boy into his pj's. The boy drifted off to sleep again as Cal pulled the covers over him. She caught a brief glance of the look on Cal's face right before he switched off the bedside lamp. The only word she could think of to describe the look was besotted.

Cal was hopelessly in love with the boy. The love showed clearly in his expression.

Her heart melted at the sight. Scotty was one lucky boy to be cared for by this uncle of his.

Cal turned and saw her standing in the doorway. He tiptoed out of the room and they walked down the hallway.

"I think I might turn in now, too. Been a long couple of days. I like to read a bit before bed." Becky Lee stopped at the doorway to her room. "Do you need anything?"

"No, I'm good. I think I'll grab a drink then I might turn in now, too. I'll be sure to be up before Scotty and make up the daybed in the sunroom."

She nodded, hoping the ruse was going to work. "I'll see you in the morning."

Cal brushed past her on the way to the kitchen, their arms barely touching. An electric jolt flashed through her, and her arm warmed at the brief touch.

She watched him walk down the hall, looking so at ease, yet out of place in her small cottage. Or maybe she was feeling out of place.

How could she feel out of place in her own cottage?

It took Cal three tries to find the cabinet with the glasses. He poured himself some cold water from the fridge and stood at the kitchen sink sipping it slowly. He felt like a man with no place of his own. A stranger in his own home. But it wasn't really his home, it was Becky Lee's. He was just a temporary visitor. His few clothes were hung in about twelve inches of Becky Lee's closet, his toiletries in the guest bathroom.

What had he done? He'd married a stranger.

He pushed the thought from his mind. It was done. He was married.

An unsettling feeling of loneliness descended upon him. The familiar stab of the loss of his brother and overwhelming responsibility of raising Scotty flowed through him.

But his next thought was relief that Becky Lee was here to help him. If nothing else, help him make decisions. He was so afraid he was going to screw something up. Raising a kid was hard work. Should he let Scotty do this or that? Was he feeding him right? Was he too young to do something that Cal thought he was old enough to do?

He'd cleaned up his language in the last few weeks, that's for sure. He was pretty sure that TJ wouldn't want Scotty learning any of the colorful language he'd been used to saying.

He set the glass in the sink and headed back to the

sunroom. As he passed Becky Lee's room he heard her moving around inside.

That feeling of loneliness crashed down on him again.

Who knew it could be so lonely living in a house filled with people?

CHAPTER 19

Greta sat on the steps of her front porch, her hands wrapped around her coffee mug like she did almost every morning. It was her favorite few moments to just be before the activities of the day took over.

A rosy pink tint crept across the early morning sky. She loved to watch the sunrise, see the subtle changes and watch until the sun popped up on the horizon. She loved the stillness, broken only by the singing of the birds as the world lightened and the day began.

She'd never been one to need an alarm and didn't quite understand the whole mentality of a snooze button, but she was grateful for her ability to wake on her own. She loved mornings, always had. The call of a cardinal drew her attention to the pine tree in the side yard, the bird's bright red feathers flashed as he landed on a branch near the trunk of the tree.

A sound drew her glance in the direction of the

drive. A car turned in and drove slowly towards the house. It wasn't Jenny or Clay's cars. She didn't recognize it. She stood up and set her coffee cup on the weathered gray planks of the porch.

The car came to a stop and the driver's car door slowly opened. A man slid out and stood there, one hand on the car door, one hand on the roof. He stared at her.

Her heart thudded in her chest, sure she was seeing a mirage. Seeing something that she'd dreamed about for so many years but never imagined would happen.

Martin.

Then she saw that grin of his spread across his face. An older face, but so familiar. He stepped away from the car, pushing the door closed and quickly crossed the distance between them.

"Greta." He paused as he stood right in front of her.

She could barely hear over the pulse pounding in her ears, and her breath came in ragged gasps.

He reached out one hand to her, and her hand, with a mind of its own, reached out to grasp his. The warmth of his strong grip fired through her. He slowly pulled her to him and wrapped her in a hug.

She leaned into his embrace, sure that if he let her go, she would fall. Her heart fluttered and for a moment, she forgot the pain and remembered only the good times.

He slowly released her and stepped back, his gaze searching her facing as if memorizing the changes. She reached up and smoothed her hair and wished she'd put on something different than the old, worn summer dress.

"You look beautiful."

"Your eyesight going bad as you age?" *She was horrible about taking compliments.*

Greta shifted back a step to look at him closely. His hair had grayed, but it had only made him more handsome. Strong muscled arms poked out of his short-sleeved knitted shirt. He had on khaki shorts and sandals and stood in the most relaxed manner as if he had no clue he'd just blown up her world.

"We need to talk." Martin looked closely at her.

The warmth of a blush flushed her cheeks. After all these years, a look from Martin could make her blush. "Well, come up on the porch and I'll go get us some fresh coffee."

Martin climbed the steps to the porch and leaned against the railing.

"I'll be right back." She hurried into the kitchen, poured two cups of coffee and made a fresh pot. She took a moment to pull herself together and try to recover from the shock. She grabbed the two cups, walked back to the front, and pushed through the screen door.

She reached to hand him his cup, and their hands brushed. A few drops of coffee splashed and she quickly pulled her hand away and swiped at the drops on her dress.

"I've got a lot to tell you. Explain to you. Do you want to sit down?"

She did want to sit down. It seemed her legs didn't

want to hold her steady this morning. She sank into a rocking chair and placed her coffee on a small table beside her. She wasn't sure of steady legs, steady hands, or steady thoughts.

Martin took a sip of his coffee. "Um, the coffee is good. I figured it was okay to come here this early. I remembered that you're an early riser."

She just sat, waiting for him to say what he had to say.

"I'm not sure where to start." He shifted on the railing, leveraging one long leg out in front to balance. "First off, about Ellie."

"I know, she's gone. Becky Lee inherited some money from her a while ago and used it to help buy the cottage she lives in."

"Well, that's the thing." He paused and looked directly at Greta. "Ellie's not gone."

Greta gasped, her hands trembled and she balled them into a fist. The grief she'd processed years ago flooded through her, mocking her. She closed her eyes for a moment, sorting out the news. She opened her eyes to see Martin kneeling beside her, his eyes filled with concern.

"I'm sorry. I didn't mean to shock you. I just wanted you to know the truth."

"But the inheritance?"

"It was all part of a plan to make it seem like Ellie had... died. To hide her better and protect her. We had some money saved, so we set a plan in motion to have Becky Lee and her siblings inherit the money. The Feds helped us set it up."

"So that's why you didn't come then. I always wondered why you didn't come back... to see me... after she died. I didn't understand what was keeping you away."

"Well, Ellie still needed me. We felt badly that her family and friends thought she was gone. But it was safer that way."

"Well, at least I know why you didn't come back. You were—are—still married to her. I understood that she was your best friend and you couldn't let her go into witness protection alone. I know your marriage to her was just to help with her new identity. But it still—hurt."

"No, I couldn't let her go into witness protection alone. I couldn't. Not after she turned over evidence against that company. Especially after what happened to her..."

"She was very brave to do that. She was. I admired her. I just didn't know that her bravery would cost me... you."

"She needed someone with her. We'd been best friends almost from the day we were both born."

"I know. She did need you. I couldn't stand for her to start a new life all alone either. I understood your choice."

Martin took both her hands in his. "But, I didn't marry her."

"What?" Greta closed her eyes for a moment. "But that was the whole reason, part of the plan."

"I know that was the plan, but... well, we pretended we were married for a while. Nothing official, just told people we were married. Then one move—at first we moved around often—we switched to telling people I was her brother. It was just... easier. I would have married her for real, like I said, to keep her safe, but the guys in witness protection said being a brother would work. Heck, I've always felt like a brother to her, so the ruse was an easy one."

"So you and Ellie aren't married? And she's alive." Greta took a moment to process all the news. "But why are you here? Isn't it making it unsafe for Ellie?"

"Someone is digging into everything. I came to warn you. I actually only have a few more minutes. Then I have to go meet someone who will whisk me away again."

"No." Her voice was barely a whisper. She reached out to touch his face. The familiar, yet older face. Clean-shaven, tanned. The familiar strong jaw. She traced a finger along his jawline.

He captured her hand and kissed it.

"Yes, I need to go. Took me forever to persuade them that I had to come here and see you, even if only for a few minutes. They're going to have a protection detail watching over Ellie's family. Covertly, of course. No one can know. But I was worried about you. I needed you to know there is some danger again. It was well known that you and Ellie were good friends. You need to keep your eyes open. Be careful."

He stood up and pulled her to her feet. She leaned against him, her head on his chest, listening to his strong heartbeat. After a minute, he pulled away slightly and bent down and kissed her. Her arms wound around his neck, and the years dropped away.

"I love you, Greta. Always have. I never stopped."

"Oh, Martin. I love you, too." She stood lost in time, wavering between memories and reality.

He stepped slowly away. "Be careful. Don't tell anyone about Ellie. That she's alive. Or that I was here."

"I won't."

He touched her cheek and brushed back a lock of her hair. "I'm so sorry, Greta. Sorry for what you had to go through. Sorry for the pain I caused. For the pain I'm causing you now. But I needed you to know there is danger… and I wanted to see you one more time. Please be careful."

She watched as he turned and walked away from her —for the second time in her life—not knowing if she'd ever see him again. Darkness enveloped her very being and she sank onto the chair, spilling the coffee on the table beside her. She stared at the drops of coffee dripping from the table to the planks on the porch. Drip. Drip. Drip.

The ever so familiar pain—the pain that she'd tried to pretend had lessened over the years—crushed her heart until she thought she couldn't breathe.

CHAPTER 20

Becky Lee and Cal pulled up to TJ's apartment in the small town near Baton Rouge. "We'll get Scotty's stuff then swing by my apartment and grab what little I have, then go see TJ."

Becky Lee slid out of the car. She looked nervous, so Cal automatically took her hand in his, squeezed it, and led the way to the apartment door. He surprised himself with his spontaneous instinct to protect her and give her courage.

He had to admit, he was a bit apprehensive himself. He didn't know if he was ready to go in the apartment again and see what he knew he'd see. He and Scotty had stayed there while they'd waited for TJ to awaken from her coma. Cal had been unable to pick up anything or change anything. His brother's running shoes would still be in the corner. His jacket and a pair of running shorts would be on the chair in his and TJ's bedroom. Loose coins would be in the jar on his brother's dresser, a habit he'd picked up as a little kid. A book he'd been reading about the stock market would be open on the bed table. All the little signs of his life.

Cal took a deep breath and slid the key in the lock and pushed open the door. He stood aside for her to enter first.

She gasped and he bumped into her back as she came to an abrupt halt.

He looked over her shoulder and let out a low whistle. "It looks like someone was searching for something."

The apartment was a mess of tumbled furniture, tossed pillows, and drawers tipped over. Becky Lee took one step into the room. "What do you think they were looking for?"

"Same thing we are? Well, not Scotty's things, but the paper TJ signed giving me custody. I'm sure my father is responsible for this."

Becky Lee crossed the room, picked up a pillow, and placed it back on the couch. She uprighted a lamp and picked up a scattered stack of mail. "I... we need to get this cleaned up."

"We do. But not today. Let's look for the document ourselves, then get some of Scotty's things. We'll come back another time and sort through all this and get it cleaned up for TJ."

He knew they had to face the mess, face picking up his brother's things, too. But he just didn't have it in him to do it now.

Becky Lee nodded. "You go pack what Scotty needs and I'll look for the document."

Cal grabbed a couple of large garbage bags and went into Scotty's room. He saw the torn up bed with the mattress flipped onto the floor and the drawers of the dresser dumped with clothes spilling everywhere. He grabbed some clothes off the floor. He randomly reached for jeans, shorts, socks, boxers, and t-shirts. The toys had mostly been left alone, so he filled a box with things he hoped Scotty would enjoy. He grabbed more of Scotty's sports stuff. He didn't really know what Scotty needed. Hoping he'd made some good choices, he hauled things out to the trunk of the car.

Two hours later they'd filled the car with clothes and toys for Scotty, but not a sign of the missing paper. Becky Lee rubbed the back of her neck. "We should go. We need to get your things and I want to see TJ."

They swung by Cal's apartment, and true to his word, he only brought out a few duffle bags and a box of books. "I travel light."

"I can see that."

They climbed in the car and he glanced over at her. Her eyes were etched with worry and she looked so tired. The last few days had been so... emotional. He reached over and touched her arm. She looked up at him with her luminous eyes shiny with unshed tears.

"I'll take you to go see TJ now."

Becky Lee stood at the side of Theresa Jean's bed. The machines were still making their ominous noises. Cal went to go talk to the doctor.

Becky Lee brushed the hair away from her sister's face. She was pale, but of course, she'd been in this bed for weeks. The room was chilly, and Becky Lee pulled a blanket up over her sister. Did her sister get cold but have no way to tell anyone? Did she have thoughts going on in her mind?

"Theresa Jean, it's time for you to wake up. You can come home with me to Comfort Crossing while you get stronger and I'll help with Scotty. He's such a great kid. You've done such a good job with him. He's got your smile, too. He misses you."

She felt Cal come and stand behind her. "Doctor said not really much change. Thinks she might be a little less deep in the coma. I talked to the doctor about moving her to the hospital in Comfort Crossing, but to be honest, he said that most likely a small community hospital like Comfort Crossing would more than likely send a patient in this condition to New Orleans or Baton Rouge or another larger city with a better facility."

"We could at least look into moving her to New Orleans. That would only be an hour away. We could see her more often."

"I think that's a good idea. We'll check into it."

"Do you think we should bring Scotty to see her again?" Becky Lee didn't know if that would be better or worse for Scotty.

"I don't know. He's settled down some. I mean, I can see he's still sad, but he's at least adjusting to his new life." Cal let out a long sigh. "I wish TJ could wake up and tell me what to do. And, as long as I'm wishing, I wish she'd tell us where that custody paper is."

Becky Lee stared at her sister, and though she might be imagining it, she thought she felt a connection with her. Which was silly because her sister was still in her coma. Becky Lee scrunched up her face, concentrating. Then her heart banged in her chest and her eyes flew open wide. "I know where the paper is."

Cal cocked his head. "Really? How?"

"I just do. Theresa Jean… *told* me. I think." Becky Lee shook her head. "I know it makes no sense. She's in a coma. But, I think the paper is in this wooden box she has. Has a carved rose on the top of it. It has a false bottom in it and she used to hide her journal there when she was a kid. We have to go back and get that box."

"I have it."

"What?"

"It was in Scotty's room. Had some trading cards in it, a deck of magic cards, a couple of foreign coins. It's in the trunk of the car."

Becky Lee squeezed her sister's hand. "Thanks, Theresa Jean. That's going to help us keep Scotty safe. Don't you worry about a thing. Just get strong and wake up." She leaned over and kissed her sister. "We're going to leave now, but I'll be back soon."

Cal leaned over Theresa Jean and whispered near her ear. "Wake up soon, sleeping beauty. We miss you. Time to get back to real life."

They left the hospital and went directly to the car. Cal dug through the trunk until he found the wooden box and held it up triumphantly.

Becky Lee took the box from him, dumped Scotty's things into a sack, and held her breath. She slid the side panel over and pressed on the carved rose on top of the box at the same time. The false bottom popped up and she saw the folded paper in the bottom. With shaking hands she took the paper out and handed the wooden box to Cal. She unfolded the paper and let out a whoop of joy.

"This is it. Look, right here. It gives you custody. It's signed and notarized." She threw her arms around Cal and hugged him. He wrapped his arms around her and leaned his head against hers. They stood for a moment enjoying the small victory before she pulled away.

Becky Lee looked Cal straight in the eyes. "See, she really was communicating with me."

"I think she probably was."

Cal dropped the signed document off at the lawyer's office on their way back from Baton Rouge. He felt like they finally had a chance against his father. Though, to be honest, his father didn't lose at much. Ever. But surely the judge would take this legal document into consideration, along with the fact he was married now, and all Becky Lee's stability.

Then why did he feel, in the pit of his stomach, that all this would still not be enough?

"What do you want for dinner?" Becky Lee interrupted his thoughts.

What did he want for dinner? What a normal, couple-ish thing to ask. "I don't care. Anything is fine."

"Let's stop by the market before we pick up Scotty. I'll see what looks good."

"I don't want you to feel like you need to feed us all the time."

Becky Lee smiled at him. "Well, I've heard about your cooking abilities, so I think I'll keep the cooking chore."

"You have to let me take over some responsibilities. I don't want you doing everything for Scotty and me."

"You can mow the yard. I hate mowing."

"I can do that. What else?"

"I'm sure we'll figure it out."

An hour later Becky Lee was busy in the kitchen, Scotty was working on his jigsaw puzzle, and Cal was mowing her yard. Sweat rolled down his chest as he pushed the old heavy mower. When all this was over and he left, he should get her a new self-propelled mower so it would be easier for her.

He stopped in his tracks. *When he left?* He was already getting used to having Becky Lee around. He realized he was in no hurry to leave, to get out of the marriage. He enjoyed Becky Lee's company. He enjoyed it a lot.

Cal reached behind his neck and shrugged off his t-shirt and used it to wipe some of the sweat away. He tucked the end of it into the back waistband of his jeans and began to push the mower again, cutting precise diagonal passes across her yard. Mowing was a good time to think. But all he could think about was Becky

Lee's blue eyes, quick smile… and how much longer all this was going to last.

~

Becky Lee heard the mower's engine turn off and glanced up at the clock. Dinner should be ready soon. Just a quick chicken and noodle casserole that she hoped Scotty would like, along with green beans—which she already knew she'd have to coax the boy to eat.

Cal pushed through the door into the kitchen and she looked up at him. Stared at him. He was standing, bare-chested, with his torso looking like it was oiled in sweat. She swallowed and told herself to quit gawking.

"I… um… dinner will be ready soon if you want to grab a quick shower." She looked away from him and busied herself with putting some rolls on a baking sheet.

She allowed herself another sideways glance his direction. He grabbed his t-shirt and swiped it over his face. He walked over to the kitchen cabinet, grabbed a glass and went to stand by the sink, filling the glass with water. He swallowed it down in a few long gulps.

His tanned back and muscled shoulders gleamed with sweat, too. She quickly looked away as he turned from the sink.

"Yep, I'll grab a shower. It sure is hot and humid out there tonight. Heard the temperature was climbing again all week."

"Really?" She'd heard that same forecast, but one-word sentences seemed the safe way to go with this shirtless version of Cal.

"I won't be long. Sure won't be using up any of your hot water. Going to take a cold shower." Cal headed out of the kitchen.

A cold shower. That actually seemed like a good idea about now.

CHAPTER 21

The court case got moved back two weeks—which made Cal think his father was up to something—but while they waited he, Becky Lee, and Scotty settled into a routine. Scotty seemed happier than he'd been in a long time. He still debated whether Scotty should see TJ again, but hated to upset the boy right now. Becky Lee was fabulous with Scotty and had changed her schedule to mostly work days so they sat down for dinner as a family most nights. The whole family dinner was such a foreign concept to him, but he found he loved the chatter at the dinner table and hearing about each person's day.

He also enjoyed helping her in the kitchen each evening. She showed him how to spin lettuce and make a salad. She'd teased him about never making a salad in his whole life. They baked cookies with Scotty and took walks after dinner or sat on the porch sipping lemonade or tea. He'd learned to make lemonade from fresh squeezed lemons.

"Can we go for a walk tonight after dinner?" Scotty looked up from his plate of fried chicken and mashed potatoes. Cal was absurdly pleased with himself for mashing the potatoes tonight. Becky Lee's teaching made cooking seem almost... easy. Not that he did any of the complicated meal prep.

"We can if we get the dishes finished first," Becky Lee bargained.

And there she was, teaching the boy chores and priorities. For about the hundredth time in a week, relief spread through him at the sharing of the responsibility of raising Scotty.

After the dishes were in the dishwasher and the leftovers put away, the three of them slowly walked along the sidewalks. Well, he and Becky Lee walked slowly. Scotty raced ahead a bit and then raced back over and over, telling them to hurry up.

Becky Lee liked to take him on a different route each time they walked, and this time as they strolled she pointed out The Feed and Seed. A man stood in the doorway and waved to her.

"Hey, Gil."

"Hi, Becky Lee," the man called out and stepped out onto the sidewalk.

Becky Lee tugged on Cal's hand. "Come on, I'll introduce you."

He looked down at her hand on his, so warm, so delicate. He let her pull him along to the doorway of the Feed and Seed.

"Gil, this is Cal… my husband."

That was the first time he'd heard her call him that and his heart pounded in his chest. *Her husband.* He stood there like a fool until Gil stretched out his hand in greeting. Cal took his hand and shook it. "Good to meet you, Gil."

"So, Becky Lee, you finally decided to settle down. Bella told me about your wedding last weekend."

Becky Lee turned to Cal. "Bella is Gil's sister."

Cal wondered if he was ever going to get everyone sorted out who he'd met in Comfort Crossing. Who was related to whom. Who dated whom. Who was a good guy, who was a bad guy—though as far as he knew, the only "bad guy" was Camille.

Scotty came racing back. "Are we going to the park, or not?"

"And this is Scotty." Cal caught himself before he said Becky Lee's nephew. They were going to tell Scotty soon, but he'd had so many changes in the last month and they hadn't found the right time.

"Hey, Scotty. Want to go in and see some puppies? A stray and her puppies decided to adopt me. They're about eight weeks old now, according to Doc Holly."

"Can I?" Scotty danced in front of Cal.

"Of course, let's go have a look." They followed Scotty and Gil inside to the back corner of the Feed and Seed. Cal had created a penned area for the dogs with a way for the mama dog to climb out if she needed a break from the pups.

"They're weaned now. Cute, aren't they?" Gil laughed as one puppy climbed over another and slid onto his back. "Doc Holly says they are Australian shepherds."

"Hey, that's what Louie is."

"Here, I'll lift you into the pen if you want to play with them." Gil scooped up Scotty and lifted him into the fenced off area.

Cal watched as Scotty laughed and rolled around with the puppies.

"Miss Becky, aren't they cool? Have you ever seen this many puppies?"

"I sure haven't." Gil shook his head. "Well, not that I've had to take care of. Doc Holly is helping me find homes, but there are these five left. Don't suppose you want a puppy?"

"Uncle Cal, can we get one? Please? Please?" Scotty jumped up with one puppy snuggled in his arms.

"Oh, I don't think so. I'm not sure Becky Lee is ready for even more creatures stuffed into her house."

"Miss Becky? Can I? I've always wanted a dog. Josh has Louie. Louie is his bestest friend. Please?"

Cal shot her an I'm-sorry glance.

Gil laughed. "Didn't mean to throw you under the bus, Bec. Bella says I'm always talking before thinking. The pups are up-to-date on their shots. I made sure of that. And the mama dog has an appointment at the vet's soon to make sure this is her last litter."

Becky Lee reached down inside the penned area and one of the puppies came up and licked her hand. "I've never had a dog either, Scotty. I don't know anything about puppies or housebreaking them or training them."

"Josh will teach me everything. I know he will."

Cal could see the exact moment she weakened. She looked into Scotty's eyes, so animated now, so happy. *Who could resist that?*

"I don't think that owning a puppy should be a quick decision." Cal tried to give her an out.

"You know what? I've always wanted a dog, too. I don't see why Scotty and I can't learn about raising a puppy together."

"You mean it?" Scotty's eyes lit up even more.

"Yes, I mean it. It's a big commitment though. A lifelong one. You'll need to feed him and walk him and take care of him."

"I will. I promise."

"You okay with this too, Cal?"

Like Cal could refuse anything these two asked him. "Looks like we'll be taking a puppy."

"Better pick out the one you want." Gil grinned. "Tell you what. I'll throw in a bag of the food I've been feeding them."

"Add in a collar and leash, too." Cal shook his head.

"And a food bowl and water bowl." Becky Lee laughed. "I think I'm as excited as Scotty. I've always wanted a dog, just never thought it was the right time. I think now is the perfect time."

"Me, too." Scotty's forehead wrinkled. "But how am I going to decide which one?"

"Sit and play with them for a bit and see if that helps." Cal had no idea how the boy would choose between all the puppies crawling over him.

"Miss Becky, come in here and you help pick."

Becky Lee stepped over the pen and sat on the floor.

One puppy came up and sat on her lap, then licked her face.

"She did that to me, too." Scotty scooted over to sit beside Becky Lee, and the puppy crawled over into the boy's lap. "I think this one likes us."

"Is she a she?" Scotty wrinkled his nose.

"That one is a girl." Gil nodded. "She's one of the calmer of the pups, but still has lots of energy."

"Her coloring is so pretty and she has gorgeous blue eyes." Becky Lee petted the pup.

"Doc Holly says she's a red merle—that's what you call her coat coloring."

"How about it? Do you like this one?" Scotty's serious expression almost made Cal laugh. Such a big decision for a little boy.

"I do." Becky Lee solemnly nodded her head then looked up at Cal and winked.

"Perfect, but now we're gonna have to pick out a name. That's gonna be hard." Scotty jumped up and tugged on Becky Lee's hand. "Let's go. I can't wait to tell Josh."

They paid for their things and slipped a collar on the puppy. Scotty hooked the leash on the collar. The dog promptly put the leash in her mouth then sat down and rolled up in it.

"I think it's going to take a bit to get her used to a leash." Becky Lee laughed.

They headed back to Becky Lee's with the puppy alternating biting the leash and tangling herself and Scotty in it until they tumbled to the ground.

After they got home, Scotty and the puppy raced around the backyard until both of them were exhausted. Cal chased Scotty into a shower and Becky Lee found Cal sitting on a rocker with the puppy sprawled across his lap, Cal mindlessly stroking the pup's head.

"She really is a cute puppy."

"You remember that when she chews her first pair of your shoes." The corner of Cal's mouth rose in a smile.

"Scotty wants the puppy to sleep in his room. What do you think?" Becky Lee sat on the rocker next to Cal and leaned over and petted the dog.

"I think we might be in for some sleepless nights, but honestly, I'd do anything for that boy."

"Me, too." Becky Lee stared out into the darkness of the night. "I hope this brings some joy back into his life. Keeps him busy while Theresa Jean has more time to heal. I know she's going to wake up soon. I can feel it."

"After the whole custody paper thing—when suddenly you knew where it was—I'm sure not going to doubt you."

"Good. Now that we have it all settled that you should always listen to me…" Becky Lee grinned. "We should go in and get Scotty to bed."

Cal stood up with the puppy in his arms, and they headed inside.

Becky Lee found an old pillow and put it down on the floor in Scotty's room for the puppy's bed. Cal propped a board up across the corner to make a temporary penned area for the pup. The puppy wanted nothing of it. She kept trying to climb over the board.

"I'll figure out something better tomorrow." Cal eyed the board.

"Can't she sleep with me?"

"I think she should have her own bed for now." Becky Lee looked at the puppy still trying to climb over the board. "She'll settle down soon."

At least Becky Lee hoped the puppy would. Otherwise, no one was getting much sleep tonight.

The puppy whined. "It's okay, girl. I'm here." Scotty sat up in bed.

"We'll give this a try for a bit. But you need to get some sleep." Cal tucked the boy back under the covers.

They left the room and sat in the kitchen, listening to the whining of the puppy. After about five minutes, she settled down. "Good. She must have been all tired out. Hope she sleeps a good long time."

"I'll listen for her. If she wakes up tonight, I'll take her outside." Cal leaned on the table and took her hand in his. "It was a really good thing you did today for Scotty."

"You remember that when you're up at two in the morning with the puppy."

They sat and talked about their new family member —the adorable, if mischievous, puppy—but Becky Lee was having a hard time staying awake. "I think I'll call it a night."

"Okay. See you in the morning."

Becky Lee walked down the hall and poked her head into Scotty's room. The boy wasn't in his bed. She looked over in the corner of the room that Cal had barricaded off for the puppy. Scotty was sound asleep on the floor, his head on his pillow, his little arm wrapped around the puppy snuggled against him. She walked into the room, got his blanket, and draped it over the sleeping duo. She stood watching the boy and the puppy, regretting fervently that her sister was missing this moment.

Cal came to the doorway and she pressed her finger to her lips in a shush sign. He nodded.

She walked out of the room with one last glance back at the boy. "We'll just break the rules for one night," she whispered to Cal.

He didn't look like he believed her for a minute.

A few nights later Becky Lee, Cal and Scotty were taking one of their after dinner walks. The still unnamed puppy was doing a bit better with leash walking. A bit. Becky Lee laughed as the puppy chased around Scotty, wrapping the leash around him as she circled.

"Stop it. You're gonna make me fall again." Scotty spun around trying to unwind. He untangled himself and took a few more steps. "Look. I found a penny." He reached down to pick up the coin.

The puppy froze, looked at him, then cocked her head to the side.

That had to be the most adorable thing Becky Lee had ever seen.

"That's it." Scotty jumped up and down.

"What?" Cal looked at the boy in confusion.

"Penny. That's her name. Penny."

The dog cocked her head to the side each time he said Penny.

"Well, then, Penny it is. Seems to fit with her copper tones in her merle coat, too." Becky Lee was glad to have a name for the puppy.

They headed toward Main Street so Becky Lee could check on her work hours for next week. As they rounded the corner on Main, Becky Lee spotted Camille and Delbert headed their way. She smothered a sigh, determined not to let the woman get to her.

Camille walked up, her hand tucked tightly against Delbert's arm. "Well, hello. You have a puppy now, too?" Camille wrinkled her nose.

"Yep. Her name is Penny. Isn't she great?" Scotty looked up at Camille.

"If you like dogs. I think they leave too much fur all over and they are so much work."

"Well, I love her and she loves me." Scotty puffed up his chest.

"Penny is a wonderful addition to our family." Cal stood with one hand on Scotty's shoulder.

Our family. A warmth rushed through Becky Lee at his words. They were kind of a ragtag family now and she liked that. She liked feeling part of a family.

"I'm sure it's nice for Scotty to live with his mother's sister and his uncle." Camille's words shot through Becky Lee and she looked quickly at Scotty.

"Cal is my uncle, but Becky Lee is his wife." Scotty stared at Camille.

"Well, and your aunt, too. Your mother's sister."

Scotty looked at Becky Lee, his eyes clouded in confusion. "You're Mom's sister?"

"Oh, I'm *so* sorry. He didn't know? How… strange. Delbert ran into Mr. Grayson who explained all about the boy." Camille didn't sound a bit sorry.

Becky Lee glared at Camille. "Nice seeing you, if you'll excuse us?" She looked pointedly at the couple until Delbert caught on and led Camille away down the sidewalk.

Becky Lee knelt beside Scotty. "Yes, I'm your aunt. I should have told you earlier, but… well, it's complicated. We were trying to keep it a secret from… someone." She looked up at Cal for help.

Cal knelt down beside Scotty, too. "It was a decision we had to make. An adult one. To keep everyone… safe."

Scotty looked right into Cal's eyes. "You mean to keep me from having to live with my grandfather?"

Cal rocked back on his heels. "What?"

"Mom told me that my grandfather wanted me to live with him and that she didn't want that to ever happen. That you'd keep me safe."

Cal wrapped the boy in a hug, the boy's little arms wound tightly around Cal's neck. "I'm doing my best, kiddo."

"So Miss Becky had to be a secret, too?"

"For a while, yes."

Scotty looked at Becky Lee from over Cal's shoulder. "So… it's okay if I know it now, though? If people know it?"

Becky Lee nodded.

"Well, can I call you Aunt Becky instead of Miss Becky?"

Becky Lee swallowed and held out her arms. The boy let loose of Cal and came over and hugged her. "I'd love it if you called me Aunt Becky."

"Hear that, Penny? I got an uncle *and* an aunt."

Cal stood up and held out his hand to help her up. She reached up to take his hand, and he pulled her effortlessly to her feet. He wrapped an arm around her —she was sure it was just for effect in case someone was watching—and they walked down the street.

Scotty bounced ahead of them, then came racing back with Penny. "Wait until I see Josh. I got a name for my dog *and* an aunt today."

Right at that moment, Becky Lee was pretty sure she was having a perfect day.

Cal leaned over and pressed a kiss against her cheek. He pulled away slightly, and she looked at the warmth in his eyes and the grin on his face. He leaned near again and kissed her on the lips.

Now she was positive it was the perfect day.

CHAPTER 22

Becky Lee took Cal's hand as they walked into the courthouse. He squeezed her hand in reply and shot her a weak smile. They stepped out of the heat and into the cool interior. Becky Lee saw their lawyer talking to another man. He finished his conversation and walked over to greet them.

"I think we have a solid case. Definitely helped by you finding the notarized document."

Becky Lee wanted the whole ordeal over. She wanted to be headed home with Cal awarded custody, and planning a celebratory dinner.

Cal's father walked up to them, flanked by a group of well-dressed, pretentious men she could only assume were his lawyers. Four of them. She swallowed hard.

"James." Cal's father greeted him. "Miss Tesson... oh, I mean Mrs. Grayson. Or is it Gray?"

"Father." Cal's voice was hard and the muscle in his jaw tightened.

"It's probably best for you two to not speak before the case." Cal's lawyer interrupted the conversation and led Cal and Becky Lee into the courtroom.

Cal and his lawyer sat at a table in front of the judge's bench, and Becky Lee slipped into a chair behind them. The lawyer and Cal had their heads together, talking quietly. She fidgeted with her watch that Cal had all set up for her.

The judge entered, and the proceedings started. Becky Lee was overwhelmed with the legal jargon as well as the harsh things Mr. Grayson's legal team said about her sister and Cal. Only they kept calling him James, and it irritated her.

She clenched her jaw and wanted to dispute everything they said. Her sister was a kind and generous person. She'd obviously done a great job raising Scotty, and he was a wonderful kid. And Cal… he loved Scotty, that was plain to see. He always had the boy's best interest at heart.

Theresa Jean, you need to wake up. Things are getting messy. She willed her sister to hear her across the miles.

Mr. Grayson's lawyer went on with his litany of Cal's shortcomings. No steady job, no money, no permanent residence, never raised a child. It didn't get any better when they turned on Theresa Jean. They even implied that she had a drug problem. Becky Lee didn't believe it for a minute.

"The doctors don't believe that Theresa Jean will come out of her coma." One of the lawyers jumped up and handed the judge some papers. "We have three doctors stating that. Too much damage has been done."

Becky Lee reeled. Her sister not wake up? That wasn't possible. It wasn't. Cal turned and glanced at her, his brow furrowed, and shook his head no.

"I have Theresa Jean's primary doctor, a specialist in neurology, the hospitalist, and two more doctors who believe her condition is improving and she's coming around." John Black handed his stack of papers to the judge.

"As you can see, James and Miss Tesson got married. How convenient," one of Mr. Grayson's lawyers remarked. "Your Honor, it was obviously just to help their case."

John Black countered, and it went on and on like this. Becky Lee tried to concentrate, but her mind insisted on wandering, avoiding the proceedings, holding out hope.

The man Becky Lee assumed was Mr. Grayson's lead attorney stood up, it caught her attention and she stared at him as he flourished some documents. "Mr. Grayson is also worried about Miss Tesson's—or is it *Mrs. Gray* now—anyway, we are worried about her other relatives. Like her aunt, Ellie Tesson. A convicted murderer."

Becky Lee sat up straight in her chair, holding her breath. What was the man talking about? Not only that, her aunt was dead. She died years ago.

The lawyer handed a stack of papers to the judge who briefly read through them.

Cal turned in his chair and looked at her, but she just shrugged her shoulders.

"We're, of course, worried that she'll return and we don't want her anywhere near the boy."

"She's dead." Becky Lee couldn't help letting the words slip out.

"No, she's very much alive. Quite possibly on the run from the law. We need a bit more time to look into all the facts, but no way should the boy be allowed to stay with James until all the facts are known." The lawyer droned on.

The court began to spin and she grabbed onto the arms of her chair. She knew her father had always refused to talk about Aunt Ellie, but this? She'd murdered someone?

But I bought the cottage with an inheritance from Aunt Ellie.

"I need time to go over all of this. We'll schedule another hearing in a week." The judge set down the papers.

"We'd like temporary custody of the boy until more permanent custody is decided."

The judge couldn't do that, could he? Take Scotty away now? She drew in a deep breath, trying to process the day and all she'd heard. Confusion coursed through her.

The judge sat silently for a moment, looked down at the papers, then looked back up. "I'll allow the boy to remain in Mr. Gray's custody for now. I'll make a final decision at the next hearing."

Becky Lee wanted to jump up and give a shout of relief, but she couldn't think. Couldn't process all she'd heard. Couldn't stand. Couldn't breathe.

∾

Cal looked back at Becky Lee and sprang to his feet. He walked back to where she was sitting and sank into the chair beside her. "Are you okay?"

"I… um… no."

He wrapped his arm around her and pulled her close. Not for show. Not to pretend they were a real couple.

Then, he realized… they *were* a real couple. He cared about her. He wanted to protect her from all the pain and the horrible things said today.

She leaned her head against his shoulder. "Theresa Jean is going to wake up, isn't she?"

"She is. That was just grandstanding on my father's part."

"But my aunt… I don't understand… she died. I got an inheritance."

He pulled her close. "I don't know about all of that. But I promise I'll help you find out the truth."

She looked up at him, her eyes filled with confusion and pain.

"They said such… mean things about Theresa Jean and you."

"I can take it. It's just my father's way. I'm sorry about the things they said about TJ, though. And there is no way she has a drug problem. No way."

John Black stopped beside them. "I'll be in touch."

Cal nodded. Their lawyer left, but he sat and held Becky Lee, waiting for her to feel strong enough to leave.

"James."

Cal looked up to see his father standing in the aisle.

"You might have gotten custody for this week but that's all you'll get. I'm going to have that boy."

"His name is Scotty," Cal said each word slowly and deliberately.

"Don't mess with me. You know I always win. One way or another."

"Is that a threat?" Cal tightened his arm around Becky Lee.

"It's more of… a promise."

His father turned and walked out of the courtroom. Cal's heart pounded in his chest. His father was a formidable foe to have. He'd put nothing past the man. Nothing at all. The man was ruthless.

"Cal?" Becky Lee's voice was low and tired.

"Yes?"

"Will you take me home now?"

"I can do that." Cal stood up and reached down with both hands. She slipped her hands in his and he pulled her to her feet.

"I want to go home and be with Scotty. Tomorrow, when I've had a bit of time to sort things out, I'm going to go talk to my father and get the truth about Aunt Ellie."

It didn't take Greta very long to decide she had to go tell Becky Lee the truth about Ellie. Becky Lee had talked to Jenny, of course, after the court case. Jenny had told Greta what happened. Now it was up to Greta to sort things out for Becky Lee.

She drove to Becky Lee's home and knocked on the door. If Becky Lee wasn't here, she'd try the Magnolia Cafe next. She heard a scuffling inside then the door opened and a puppy jumped up on her, nearly bowling her over.

"Penny. Bad dog. Don't jump on people." Scotty reached out grabbed a shoe from the puppy's mouth. "I'm sorry. I'm trying to teach her not to do that." The boy looked at the shoe. "Penny, Aunt Becky is going to be so mad when she sees what you did to her shoe."

Greta reached down to greet the dog. "Hello there, Penny. Looks like Scotty has his work cut out training you."

"You know me?"

"My daughter-in-law is a friend of Becky Lee's."

"Oh. Did you know she's my aunt?"

"I did."

"Well, I know now, too. She's a pretty cool aunt."

Becky Lee came up behind the boy. Her face was creased with worry, her eyes red from tears or lack of sleep... or maybe both. "Hi. What brings you here? Everything okay with Jenny? I just talked to her last night."

"We need to talk for a bit. It's important."

"We could have tea on the back patio if you'd like."

"I'd like that." Greta stepped inside.

"Scotty, why don't you work on your puzzle while I visit with Greta?"

"Okay, but I hope Penny doesn't try to eat any more puzzle pieces." Scotty let out a long-suffering sigh.

Becky Lee poured two glasses of tea and led the way

out back. Greta sat down beside her, wondering where to start.

"I need to tell you some things. Things that have been secret for years. It looks like everything is unraveling now, so I'm going to tell you the truth. You see, your Aunt Ellie and I were best friends growing up."

"You were? I didn't know." Becky Lee brushed her hair back behind her shoulder. "In court they said she was alive. How can that be? I inherited money from her. I don't even know why she ever left. My father won't talk about it."

"It's a long story. But, I did recently learn that indeed Ellie is alive. They faked her death to try to keep all of you safer. Keep Ellie safer."

"So that's the truth? She's alive?"

"It is. Ellie has been in hiding for all these years. She's actually in witness protection."

"Really? They said she murdered someone."

"I wouldn't call it murder, but someone did get killed. It was self-defense. She was..." Greta paused and took a deep breath. It was still hard to think about it all these years later. "Ellie was attacked by someone she worked with. She fought the man and smashed a large urn over him while she was fighting him off. He fell and struck his head on the corner of his desk."

"Poor Ellie had a black eye, sprained wrist, and was so very scared."

"But why did she have to hide?"

"There was this overly ambitious prosecutor. He said they could press murder charges against Ellie. They wouldn't press charges if she got evidence against her employer. It wasn't fair because she was only protecting herself. But she was afraid she'd go to jail. She got the evidence they needed and testified. Then her life was threatened… and everyone in her family. So they put her in witness protection."

"All alone?"

"Well, no. A good friend of hers, Martin, went into the program with her a little bit later, after spreading the word he was leaving town and moving to California. Martin and Ellie grew up together. They were friends since, well, forever. He couldn't let her go off and start a new life all alone. So, he went with her. The Feds weren't happy, but by now it was coming out that the prosecutor wasn't on the up and up. He had not so much offered a plea bargain, as illegally threatened her to get the evidence he needed."

"So, she's still hiding?"

"She is. But now, somehow, some of the information is coming out. Cal thinks his father has something to do with it. He has very powerful connections."

Greta looked out at Becky Lee's garden. "You need to be extra careful now. Watch out for anything suspicious. She messed with a powerful family. There are actually some agents around town keeping an eye on you and your family."

"Watching me?"

"Yes, just to make sure nothing happens."

"So, by marrying Cal, I've put Scotty and him in danger?"

"I… well, I don't know, dear."

Becky Lee stood up and paced. "I've messed

everything up. I was just trying to do the right thing for Scotty. Now, I've made it worse. Much worse."

"You made the choice you did for the right reason. You didn't know. I didn't know that Ellie was even alive when you married."

"I guess this is why father never talked about Ellie. Did he think she was a murderer and just ran away?"

"I think Ellie told him the truth but warned him not to tell anyone, to keep you all safe."

"So that's why he wouldn't talk about her and always changed the subject." Becky Lee stopped pacing. "Oh, I should go and tell him that Ellie is alive. He thinks she's dead, too."

"I don't know how all this is going to end. I don't know who dug into this, or why. Maybe it was Cal's father. I don't know. I do know you all need to be careful."

Becky Lee turned to Greta. "Thank you for coming here and explaining all this to me. We will be careful. I'll go talk to Cal right away. We'll keep an even closer eye on Scotty."

"I'm sorry you're in the middle of all these troubles now. You need to have faith that things will work out the way they were meant to."

"I'm just hoping we're all meant to be safe."

CHAPTER 23

As soon as Cal got home from work, Becky Lee led him out to the front porch while Scotty played with Penny in the backyard. He listened while she explained everything that Greta had told her.

He sat quietly as she told the whole story, holding her hand and listening, giving her strength.

"So, you see, I've only made it worse for you, marrying you. Now Scotty might be in danger because of me. Because of my family. I was just trying to keep him safe and look what a mess I've made."

"You haven't made a mess. You had no way of knowing any of this." Cal rubbed his jaw. "It looks like we're going to have to be even more careful now."

"I know. Greta said they have people watching us. That's kind of creepy, isn't it?"

"Not if it keeps Scotty safe. I think we might need to adjust our work schedules for a while though. I'd feel better if Scotty was with you or me."

"That's a good idea. I'll talk to Keely. Take some time off. It's the least I can do. I've just... I've made everything so much worse."

"No, you haven't." Cal leaned in and took both her hands in his. He needed her to know how he felt. "These weeks have been the happiest of my life. I mean, I miss Gordon and I'm sad about him. I'm worried about TJ. But being married to you and having Scotty with us. Best thing ever."

He looked into her eyes. "I've been wanting to do this for the longest time."

He tilted her chin up and leaned in and kissed her lips. A long, lingering kiss. Not for anyone's benefit but their own. She kissed him back and wrapped her arms around his neck. He placed one hand on her soft, warm cheek.

He finally pulled back slightly and she dropped her arms to her side.

"That was just for us." He grinned at her. "Did you like the real thing?"

"I... did." A sweet smile spread across Becky Lee's face. "I liked it a lot. I might even like another one."

"As you wish, ma'am." He stood up and pulled her to her feet. He leaned down and kissed her again, wrapping his arms around her slender body, pulling her close until his thoughts were tangled in wanting and giving and knowing he was falling for this woman.

Heck, he'd already fallen for her.

What kind of mess had he gotten himself into? He'd fallen for a woman who had married him just to keep her nephew safe.

Becky Lee tried to collect her thoughts as Cal finally released her. She reluctantly pulled back, wanting to touch her lips where his kiss still haunted her.

"We should go in and get supper ready, I suppose. Scotty's probably starving. He's always starving." Cal's practical words brought her out of the haze of his kisses.

"Growing boy." Becky Lee turned, pulled open the screen door, and paused. "Cal, I'll make it up to you and Scotty. I will."

"I told you, none of this is your fault."

She walked into the house with Cal right behind her. She went to the fridge and opened the door, her mind muddled, and for once she had no idea what she was going to make for dinner.

Cal crossed to the back door and looked out. "Scotty?" He stepped outside. "Scotty?"

Becky Lee heard the change in his tone of voice and closed the refrigerator and walked to the door. "What's the matter?"

"Scotty's not here." Panic edged Cal's voice.

Becky Lee scanned the small backyard. It's not like there was anywhere to hide. "Scotty."

She came up beside Cal and grabbed his arm. "Look, the gate is open."

They hurried over to the gate and looked in each direction. No sign of the boy.

"I'm going to look out front." Cal turned and headed toward the front yard.

Becky Lee stood frozen for a moment, fear cascading

against her, hammering her with guilt. Greta had told her to be careful. What if whoever was after her Aunt Ellie got Scotty? Why had they let him play outside alone? That was just… unforgivable.

She ran around to the front yard and saw Cal coming back down the street. "I don't see him anywhere." Cal raked his hand through his hair.

"Let's split up. I'll go towards Main Street, you go that direction. I'll grab my cell. Call me if you find him."

Cal nodded.

She looked up at the darkening sky. Thunder rumbled in the distance. The breeze picked up suddenly and she could smell the rain in the air. It was not a good time for a storm. They needed to find Scotty and find him fast.

Cal loped off down the street, calling Scotty's name.

She raced inside and for once found her cell phone immediately. She snatched it off the kitchen table and hurried toward Main Street. A loud crash of thunder and a flash of lightning cracked through the sky. Ever since the tornado, she'd made sure she was safely inside somewhere if a storm came in, but tonight she had to find Scotty.

Twenty minutes later she'd walked down Main Street and stuck her head in any open business, asking if they'd seen Scotty. A large plop of rain splashed on the sidewalk. Then another. She looked up at the gray sky. Ominous dark clouds rolled in from the distance.

Another crash of thunder made her jump. Her

phone rang and she snatched it out of her pocket. "Did you find him?"

"No, you didn't have any luck either?"

"I'm going to call Sheriff Dawson and let him know that Scotty is missing. Just in case he or his deputies see him."

"Good idea. It looks like it's going to storm any minute."

"We have to find him." Becky Lee could hear the panic in her voice.

"We will." Cal's voice was low but had an underlying tone of panic matching her own.

"I'll call the sheriff. Maybe we should meet back home? Maybe he's back there."

"Good idea. I'll meet you there." The phone went dead in her hand. She dialed the sheriff and explained the situation then headed back to her house, stopping at more businesses on the way.

The rain let loose before she made it home. It poured in cold angry drops, pelting and soaking her. Her clothes clung to her and her hair hung in wet clumps. She raced for her home, hoping against hope that Scotty would be there.

Cal stood on the front porch and watched as Becky Lee came running down the street in the pouring rain. She looked like a bedraggled doll that some child had left out in the storm. She stepped up on the porch, out of breath.

"He's not here?"

"No." Cal's heart pounded in his chest and fear gripped him. He'd promised TJ he'd keep Scotty safe. He reached for Becky Lee, but she stepped away. "I'm going to go put on some dry clothes. I'll make some phone calls, too."

"I'm going to go back out looking." Cal didn't know where to look, but he knew he couldn't just stand here and do nothing.

"Let me get you an umbrella. Not that it will do much good in this storm."

As if in agreement, thunder crashed again, shaking the house.

Cal grabbed a jacket and the umbrella and headed back out into the storm. He walked up and down street after street, calling Scotty's name. The rain soaked his clothes and shoes. At one point he stood under a big elm tree when the sky started to pelt down hail. Each ping of hail reminded him he hadn't kept Scotty safe. What was Scotty doing in the storm? Had he found shelter? Was he out in this hail?

Had his father taken him? That was his biggest fear. His father would stop at nothing. Then he realized that wasn't his biggest fear. He'd no idea if his father had snatched him, or worse yet, maybe it was whoever was after Becky Lee's aunt. How could he have failed Scotty so spectacularly?

Just then his phone rang. He grabbed it from his pocket. "Hello?"

"Cal? This is Gil. From the Feed and Seed. I have Scotty here with me."

His heart soared and he dropped to his knees in relief, no longer able to stand. "Is he okay?"

"He's fine. Found him out back under some wood I had leaned against the building. He's pretty soaked, but I have him inside getting warmed up."

"I'll be right there." Cal stood up, heedless of the hail, and raced down the street. He stopped for a moment beneath another tree and dialed Becky Lee.

"He's at the Feed and Seed with Gil."

"I'll be right there." Becky Lee's voice choked.

He ran the rest of the way to the store and pushed through the front door. A bell jangled overhead. He stood dripping in the doorway. Gil handed him a towel. "Here. Looks like you can use this. Scotty's in the back with Penny and her mom."

Cal walked to the back of the store, taking deep breaths to calm down. He spotted Scotty sitting with Penny and her momma dog, and his eyes filled with tears. He stood for a moment and choked back the tears filling his eyes. Scotty was safe. That was all that mattered.

"Hey, kiddo." Cal walked over and knelt down beside the boy and the dogs. Penny jumped up and licked his face.

"Uncle Cal, Penny got out the gate and ran down the street. I ran after her to catch her, but then I got *lost-ed*. I think Penny wanted to see her mom though. I think she misses her…" Scotty's voice cracked. "Just like I miss my mom."

Cal sat on the floor, pulled Scotty into his lap, and

wrapped his arms around the boy. "I know you do. I'm sorry I can't fix it for you."

"But you're gonna make it so I don't have to go live with my grandfather, right?" Scotty looked up at Cal, his eyes bright with worry.

"I am trying my best, kiddo." Cal hugged the boy closer. "But you know, you can't go running off like that. Even if Penny gets out. You come get me or Becky Lee, okay? We were so worried."

"I was worried, too. It got dark with the storm and I couldn't figure out which street was the way home. Then Penny led me here, but I couldn't get the door open to the store."

Gil came over and handed them two steaming mugs. "Hot chocolate. Figured it might help warm you two up. Good thing I came back tonight to get my laptop. When I pulled in, I saw Penny in the headlights. Brought them both inside and called."

Cal stood up and shook Gil's hand. "I can't thank you enough."

The bell jangled in the front of the store and Becky Lee came rushing over. She leaned down and scooped Scotty into a hug. "Oh, Scotty. You're okay." She stroked his hair, holding him close. Tears streamed down her face and she did nothing to hide them. She stepped back with a hand on each of his shoulders and looked at him closely. "You are okay, aren't you?"

"I'm fine, Aunt Becky. Just wet. I think Penny wanted to visit her mom. I want to visit my mom, too."

Cal looked at Becky Lee, who nodded.

"Okay, kiddo. I'll take you to see her tomorrow. She's still… sleeping, but we'll go see her."

"You hear that Penny? I get to see my mom, too."

Becky Lee watched as Cal picked up the boy in his arms and carried him out to her waiting car. She followed behind them. Scotty buried his face in Cal's neck. Cal held the boy close, murmuring assurances in his ear.

She'd swear her heart swelled in her chest at that very minute. These two, she cared about them so much. She was pretty sure a finer man had never been born than Cal Gray. She drove them home and watched as Cal got a sleepy Scotty out of the car. He carried him to his bedroom, shucked off the boys wet clothes and helped him into his pajamas.

Penny jumped up on the bed and settled down next to Scotty. *Well, it couldn't hurt, right?* Just this one night the dog could sleep on the bed.

Cal sat on the edge of the bed, brushed Scotty's hair from his face, and leaned over and kissed the boy's cheek. He sat there quietly, watching as Scotty drifted off to sleep. Cal's face was cloaked in low light from the bedside lamp. His strong jaw was etched into the shadows. A day's worth of whiskers darkened his cheek. Scotty's small hand clutched Cal's.

Cal continued to sit on the bed, not moving. Becky Lee couldn't pull herself away from the doorway, so both of them stayed and watched the boy sleep. Finally, Cal slowly stood up and walked towards her. She would swear electricity crackled through the room between them.

At least she could feel it. It stabbed through her like a bolt of lightning, shocking her, numbing her... and making her feel so alive at the same time.

He stood close to her and touched her face. She reached up and covered his hand. They stood in silence for she didn't know how long. She wanted him to kiss her. She should kiss him. But that wasn't really part of their agreement, was it?

Though he had kissed her once when no one was around.

The thoughts tumbled through her head and she didn't quite have the nerve to stand on tiptoe and kiss him.

Coward.

Cal pulled away and the spot on her face, where his hand just was, felt empty and cold.

"We should probably call it a night." Cal scrubbed his hand over his face and his rough whiskers.

"Yes, we should." But she didn't want that. She didn't want to go into her lonely room by herself, didn't want to be away from him.

Cal walked down the hall, and a chasm of loneliness filled her. She stepped into her room and closed the door softly. She leaned against the door and stared at her bed. How did things get so messed up? She knew that Cal would be on his way as soon as Theresa Jean woke up. Go back to his nomad lifestyle. Pop in to see them every once in a while. He was probably counting the days until he got his freedom back. Counting the days when he wouldn't be saddled with so much responsibility. Well, she was going to do nothing to stop him. He'd given up so much for Scotty. He deserved to get his life back as soon as he could.

CHAPTER 24

The next morning Becky Lee felt slightly guilty that she was making fried biscuits rolled in cinnamon sugar for Scotty's breakfast. She'd been really good about healthy meals, but she remembered how much she'd loved the fried biscuits when she was a child.

Cal and Scotty waded into the tantalizing breakfast. She swore the two of them never stopped eating.

"This is the best breakfast ever." Scotty reached for another biscuit.

Becky Lee heard a knock at the front door. "I'll get it. You guys keep eating."

She opened the door to see Sheriff Dawson standing in the doorway. "Hi, Mark. Did you come to check on Scotty? He's fine. Doing great this morning."

"No, sorry Becky Lee, I'm here on official business."

"What is it?" Becky Lee could feel her forehead crease.

"Is Cal here?"

"Yes, he's eating breakfast."

"Could you get him for me?"

Becky Lee hurried back to the kitchen and motioned for Cal to come with her.

He got up from the table. "Be right back, kiddo."

They walked to the front door.

"Cal, this is Mark Dawson, the sheriff." Becky Lee stood at Cal's side, wondering what this was all about.

"I hear you wanted to talk to me."

"There is no other way to put this, Mr. Gray. I have a warrant for your arrest."

Becky Lee's eyes flew open wide. "What are you talking about? Arrest him. Why?"

"It's an outstanding warrant that was brought to our attention. I have to take him in." Mark looked uncomfortable but sure in doing his sworn duty.

"This is probably my father's doing. I told you I'd put nothing past him. He's trying to up his odds of getting custody. I'll call John Black and get this sorted out."

"But this isn't right."

Cal put his hand on her arm. "It'll be okay."

Becky Lee didn't feel so sure. She knew that Cal's father had managed to get his brother thrown in jail for something he hadn't done.

Scotty came up behind them. "Uncle Cal?"

Cal knelt beside the boy. "I have to go with the sheriff for a bit."

"But you were taking me to see my mom today." Scotty's lips trembled.

Cal looked up at Becky Lee. "Can you go ahead and

take him?"

"But I should stay and help you get this sorted out."

"There isn't anything you can do. I'll talk to the lawyer."

Becky Lee nodded. "Okay, Scotty and I will go see Theresa Jean. Then we'll come right back here."

"I should have it sorted out before you get back."

Becky Lee hoped so but didn't trust Cal's father. He was a powerful and ruthless man, that much she'd come to believe.

Cal leaned close and brushed a kiss against her forehead. "I'll be back soon."

He walked out to the sheriff's car. To her surprise, Mark started to put handcuffs on Cal. She quickly turned Scotty away from the sight.

"Aunt Becky? Is everything okay with Uncle Cal?"

"He just has a few things to deal with. How about you finish your breakfast, and we'll go see your mother?"

"What about Penny?"

"She can't go to the hospital. I'll call Jenny and see if she can stop by and check on Penny while we're gone."

"Is she good with dogs?" Scotty's face was etched with concern.

Becky Lee had to keep from smiling. "She is. She has a dog of her own, Choo Choo."

"Okay then, I guess that will work." Scotty headed back toward the kitchen.

Unease settled over Becky Lee. She had a sense that she couldn't shake that things were starting to unravel. An instinct or a premonition or just a gut feeling. She always listened when her intuition spoke to her. She was going to have to be very careful and alert. Something was headed her way. She could feel it.

～

Later that morning, Becky Lee held Scotty's hand as they walked into Theresa Jean's room. The boy clung tightly to her, walking with short, tentative steps.

He glanced at the machines beside his mother's bed, then walked up to stand beside her. "Mom, it's me. Scotty."

He turned to Becky Lee. "Can she hear me?"

"Probably. I think so anyway."

"Mom, can you wake up? I miss you." Scotty's eyes filled with tears. He took his mother's hand. "I really wish you'd get better and wake up. You know what? I got a dog. Penny. You'll let me keep her, won't you? You always said I could have a dog when I got older. I'm a lot older now, Mom. You've been asleep forever."

Becky Lee stood behind Scotty, watching her sister carefully for any sign she was hearing her son.

"Hey, I think she squeezed my hand." Scotty looked at his mom. "Did you squeeze my hand?"

Becky Lee stared at Theresa Jean's hand in Scotty's but saw no sign of any motion.

"She did, Aunt Becky. Really."

They stayed and talked to Theresa Jean for over an hour. Scotty told her all about what he'd been up to and all about Penny.

"We probably should go now and let your mom rest." Becky Lee could see that the visit was tiring Scotty.

He'd been so hopeful he could get his mother to wake up.

"Can we come back soon?"

"Yes, we'll bring you back soon, I promise." Becky Lee wanted to get back to Comfort Crossing and see what was going on with Cal and see if she could help.

Scotty kissed his mother's cheek. "Bye, Mom. I'll be back soon, okay? Or you could wake up and come home. That would be the best thing."

She kissed her sister and whispered in her ear, "Take care, sis. It's time for you to wake up. I need you."

Becky Lee took Scotty's hand in hers and they walked out of the room, out of the hospital, and into the fresh air outside. She took a deep breath. They headed across the parking lot when two men came out of nowhere and flanked them on each side. One man leaned close to her ear and grabbed her arm. "Come with us. Don't scream and no one gets hurt."

Becky Lee clutched Scotty's hand in hers looking around wildly for help. There was no one in the parking lot. *How did that happen in a busy hospital?*

The men led them towards a plain white van. They stopped by it and one man opened the back door. "Get inside."

"Aunt Becky?" Scotty looked up at her, confused.

"It's okay. We're going to go for a little ride."

Scotty climbed in the van, and the man took Becky Lee's purse as she climbed in after him. He looked through it, pulled out her cell phone, showed his partner, then dropped it back into the purse. They took the purse with them, then the van doors slammed shut.

"Aunt Becky. It's dark." Scotty's voice floated across the blackness.

She reached out until she could feel him. "Let's sit down. Your eyes will get adjusted to the darkness soon, and you'll be able to see me."

She sat down and tucked the boy close to her side, trying to think rationally. Trying to devise a plan, a way to escape.

She didn't know who had taken them and didn't know if it scared her more if all this was something Cal's father had done or if it had something to do with Aunt Ellie. She did know her heart was banging in her chest as she tried to stay calm for Scotty's sake. She also knew that she wasn't doing a very good job on the stay-calm part.

She pressed the button on her watch so it would light up and she could see the time. She wanted to time how long the van ride was to help her figure out where they were.

As she pushed the button, she gasped. She did have a way to get help.

Cal sat in the sheriff's office, sipping coffee, trying to process all that the three men sitting in front of him had said.

"So, I'm not under arrest?"

"No, that was just to get you to come here. And if anyone was watching, it would look legit." The one man Cal thought was the leader leaned against the table. "We need your help if we're going to catch your father this time."

"What's he up to this time? Tax fraud? Laundering money?"

"He's actually helping out another man we've been investigating. Luca Abelli."

"Abelli." He knew the name. That's the name of the man who Becky Lee's aunt had put in jail. He'd no idea on how much these men knew about that and wasn't going to talk until he knew more about what they wanted from him. He was still annoyed over his "arrest."

"Your wife's aunt turned evidence on Franco Abelli. Luca is his son."

"How did my father find out about the Abelli family?"

"We think we have a leak somewhere. Looks like the Abelli family took their time to seek revenge and found someone to pay to give them information."

"How can I help with this?"

"We'd like you to visit your father and wear a wire. See if you can get him to talk."

"Wear a wire? Like in some kind of gangster movie?" Cal leaned back in his chair. "My father and I rarely speak. The last time we did, he threatened me. Why do you think he'd actually tell me anything?"

"You might be able to shake him up. Catch him off guard."

"My father is never caught off guard. No one ruffles his feathers. Believe me."

"Our research says you appear to be the only one who can get under his skin."

Okay, he'd agree with that assessment. He and his father had gotten into their share of screaming matches. He did seem to be able to rile his father. He still didn't give the agent an answer.

"Are you saying you won't help?" The agent stared at Cal.

"I'm saying I'll think about it. My father isn't really a man I want to cross. I prefer to stay out of his line of fire."

"If we arrest him, he won't get custody of your nephew." Another agent sat down across from him.

Cal scrubbed his hand across his chin. Now that was a powerful motivator to help them. He had no love lost with his father, and maybe this would be one way to protect Scotty for good.

The lead Fed guy came over and handed him a card. "Think about it. We'll be in contact."

"So I'm free to go now?" Cal looked over at Sheriff Dawson.

"You are."

Cal got up from the table and walked out of the room, out of the sheriff's office, and away from the decision he had to make. He emerged into the glaring sunshine of the early afternoon. Okay, he'd already decided he'd help... he just wasn't ready to tell the agents yet. He was still ticked off about the arrest. His father was long overdue to be caught at one of his illegal activities. This was a way to keep Scotty safe, not to mention that his father had let Gordon go to jail for something he hadn't done.

Cal felt like he should feel guilty about helping to

get his father locked up. But he didn't. He did, however, feel guilty about *not* feeling guilty.

He was surprised, and yet not, that his father had gotten involved with the son of the man who Becky Lee's aunt had put in jail. He hoped that this time they could catch his father and stop him.

He reached into his pocket to get his cell phone to call Becky Lee and realized he must have left it on the kitchen table at home. He loped the distance back to the house, hoping that Becky Lee and Scotty would already be back from visiting TJ.

Becky Lee's car wasn't there, and he walked into the empty house. Penny greeted him by jumping on him, of course. She also had a chewed up shoe of Becky Lee's in her mouth. Cal snagged the shoe and shook his head. Becky Lee was going to run out of shoes at this rate. He let Penny out into the backyard and searched for his phone. He saw it on the counter and snatched it up.

Nothing, no messages. No missed calls. As he got ready to call Becky Lee, a text message came through. He clicked on it to open it.

White van. License 2AB0429

It was from Becky Lee. What did that mean? Before he could answer her another text came in.

AL tags. Help. Kidnapped. Don't call or text back.

His pulse pounded and he clutched the phone. He grabbed a card from his pocket and tapped in the number one of the Federal Agents had given him.

"Cal Gray here. I need help. They have Becky Lee and Scotty."

CHAPTER 25

Becky Lee held Scotty tight after she'd texted Cal, using her watch, the watch that she'd thought had been a silly gift since she was not a techie person. But she'd spoken into it like some kind of spy gadget, and off her texts had gone. Now, if only her captors didn't look at her cell and know she'd sent them. Could they tell she'd sent them? She wasn't sure how all this worked, but at least Cal would have the license number. If he got the text…

The van pulled to a stop and she glanced at her watch. A little over an hour of driving. She tried to figure out what was within an hour of Baton Rouge.

"Aunt Becky, the van stopped. Do you think… they are going to shoot us?" Scotty whispered in the darkness.

"Of course not. That's only in the movies." Her heart pounded and she squeezed him tight.

"Maybe they want ransom money. Only Mom isn't awake to pay them."

"It will be okay."

The van doors opened. "Get out."

She and Scotty scooted to the door and climbed out. Scotty clung to her arm. She glanced around and it looked like they were in some kind of warehouse.

Somewhere.

"Over that way." The man nodded towards their left.

She started walking that way slowly, looking around for something, anything she could use as a weapon, or some route to escape. They walked a long distance, she'd swear it was almost as long as a football field. She wondered what the warehouse had been used for, it was clearly abandoned now.

They got to the far wall and the man tugged open a heavy wooden door with a way too sturdy-looking sliding bolt lock on it. "In there. And if you know what's good for you, you won't make any noise."

She and Scotty stepped inside, and the door banged shut behind them. She heard the sound of the lock being clicked closed. She looked around the room in the dim light. Far above them, way out of reach, was a small window with a grate over it. The room had a few boxes and chairs, and an old desk.

As soon as she heard the man walk away, she pushed the button on her watch. No luck. She was too far away from her cell phone for it to connect to send another message.

Becky Lee let her eyes adjust to the low light. The window was up high, too high for her to even boost Scotty up to it. She opened one of the boxes. It was filled with glass water bottles like the kind in water dispensers. Unfortunately, they weren't filled with water, either. Surely the men would come back soon and give them water and food?

"Aunt Becky? They aren't going to just leave us in here forever are they?"

"No. They'll let us out." She hoped she wasn't lying to the boy.

She opened another box in the corner, and it was filled with packing material.

Not helpful. Not helpful at all.

"What are you looking for?"

"Something I might be able to use to get us out of here."

"I'll help you look." Scotty went over to a stack of boxes and opened the first one. "It's got stacks of paper in it."

Becky Lee tugged open the drawer on the desk. Maybe she could move the desk over to the wall below the window. It still wouldn't be high enough to reach the window. She wondered if the men were far enough away she could try scooting it without them hearing her.

She glanced over at Scotty who was tugging on the stack of boxes. Suddenly the stack of boxes tumbled to the floor. Scotty jumped out of the way, just in time.

She turned to watch the door, sure the men would burst in here after all the commotion, but nothing. She got up and went to stand by Scotty. "You sure you're okay?"

"Come help me. We're going to quietly move that desk to the wall, okay? I'll stand on it and see how close we can get to the window."

The desk was an old, sturdy wooden desk and heavier than an elephant as far as Becky Lee could tell. She leaned against it and pushed. It moved maybe an inch.

"I'll help." Scotty pushed with her.

The desk slid another inch or so. Great, in about twelve hours they'd have it moved. She stood up and stared at the desk, willing it to be lighter.

Hope sprang up inside her. "The drawers. We'll take out the drawers." She tugged on them and placed each one on the floor. She realized if they stacked the drawers on top of the desk, they'd get more height that way, too. She dumped the contents of the drawers on the floor.

She and Scotty shoved the desk across the floor, slowly and steadily, trying not to make any noise. They placed it under the window, then Becky Lee stacked the three drawers on top of the desk. She climbed up on her makeshift ladder. She was so close.

She scanned the room, looking for something else to use. She saw an old wooden file cabinet in the corner of the room. *Bingo.*

They repeated their process of pulling out drawers, then shoved the file cabinet over to the desk. They leveraged it on top of the desk, and the two of them grabbed the cabinet and upended it to stand upright.

"Stand back in case all this topples over." Becky Lee used the desk drawers to get on top of the four-drawer file cabinet. She could see out the window now. Her heart dropped when she realized the grate on the window was screwed in place. She tugged on it, but it didn't budge. All this work for nothing. She climbed down to the floor.

"You can't get the window open?"

"The grate is covering it. It's screwed in place. I need to find something to get it unscrewed." She walked over to contents of the desk scattered on the floor. A small metal ruler, that might work. A letter opener. She shuffled through the mess.

"Look." Scotty held up a screwdriver.

She leaned over and kissed him. "You're my hero."

She scrambled off the floor and climbed back up to the window. Each screw fought back but she finally won. She held her breath and tugged on the grate.

It didn't budge.

"Listen you stupid grate. I didn't do all this for you to just stick there." She tugged on it again and the bottom of it swung loose. Then, to her surprise, she was holding it in her hand. She turned the lever on the window and it swung open. She looked down and saw a closed dumpster below the window.

This was going to work.

Her heart raced and she was afraid the men would return at any moment. She climbed down to the desktop. "Scotty, I'm going to help you climb up here. You're going to go out the window and I'm going to hold your hands and let you down as far as I can. You'll have to drop the rest of the way. Can you do that?"

"I can do it. I can."

She helped him climb up on top of the file cabinet, and she stood carefully behind him. She grabbed the windowsill with one hand and held her other hand down for Scotty to step into. She boosted him up until he could wiggle out onto the window frame. He swung one leg outside.

"Okay, I'm going to squeeze up here with you and hold onto your hands. I'll lower you as far as I can." Scotty wiggled out the window and hung on. She rested her stomach on the window sill, grabbed both his hands and lowered him as far as she could.

"Okay, I'm going to let go. You still have about four or five feet to drop to the dumpster."

"I'm ready. Let go."

She shut her eyes briefly. *Theresa Jean, look after your son.* She opened her eyes and let go. The boy dropped to the dumpster. He stood up and gave her the thumbs up.

Now, she just had to lower herself as far as possible and drop. Scotty had climbed down to the ground, out of the way. She wiggled and pushed off the file cabinet to get out the window. Her movements sent the file cabinet and drawers crashing to the ground. In a panic she wriggled through the window, lowered herself outside, and held onto the window opening. She looked below.

You're going to be fine. Becky Lee swore she heard Theresa Jean's voice. She let go and dropped down onto the dumpster, hoping she didn't break anything. She landed with a thud, lost her balance, and fell on her rear. She didn't have time to stop. She sat up and climbed off the dumpster.

She took Scotty's hand in hers, glanced quickly both directions, flipped a coin in her head and chose left. They raced off down the street and dodged into the nearest alley, hoping if the men ran outside if they heard the crashing noise, they wouldn't see which way she and Scotty had headed.

By some kind of magic that Cal thought only happened on TV shows, the Feds had picked up the van. They knew it had gone into a warehouse district near New Orleans. He'd ridden with them, after a brief argument and not taking no for an answer.

It seemed like the trip took forever. He stared at his phone, willing Becky Lee to text again, let him know they were okay. He clenched his jaw, choking back the anger that raged against his father. Was he involved in all of this?

His mind went through all kinds of terrible scenarios. Was Scotty frightened? He bet Becky Lee was putting on a good front for the boy, pretending everything was going to be okay. But was it? Had they been hurt?

He glanced at his watch as they approached New Orleans. They'd sped the distance from Comfort Crossing to New Orleans in record time, with sirens blazing until they got near the area.

The driver parked the car in an alleyway. Two other cars pulled up behind them. A handful of men came up to talk to the lead agent. "It's the warehouse three blocks down. Has a big red door on Morgan Street. A back door on Fifth. We'll split up and come at it from front and back."

The agent turned to Cal. "You stay by the car. We'll handle this. We don't want you jeopardizing anything. Got it?"

Cal nodded. He didn't want to put the operation at risk. They knew what they were doing, right? He leaned against the side of the car watching the agents head off down the street. That lasted all of about five minutes until he couldn't stand it any longer.

Cal hurried after the agents, keeping his distance.

He slipped down the street, ducking into alleys and doorways, staying back. He saw the warehouse in the next block and went down a side street to get near it.

Shots rang out and his heart tripped. Scotty and Becky Lee were in there. They shouldn't be shooting. What were they thinking? A side door was ajar near him and he slipped inside.

"Freeze."

Cal stood absolutely still.

"Oh, for Pete's sake. It's you. You almost got yourself killed." The lead agent lowered his gun.

"Are Becky Lee and Scotty safe? Who the heck was firing guns with them in here?" Cal let his anger and fear loose on the agent.

"I'm afraid they aren't here."

"What do you mean?"

"It appears that Becky Lee got them out. From a window high up in a room they were locked in." The agent's voice held a tinge of admiration. "Unfortunately, one of the men that kidnapped them is still missing. I assume he's out looking for them."

Cal struck the door frame with the palm of his hand.

"We did get the other kidnapper and we got Luca. We even have his conversation with the thug he hired, incriminating himself with ordering the kidnapping. That's been a long time coming, taking down Luca."

"Fine, you got your guy. Now we need to find Becky Lee and Scotty. We need to find them before the other kidnapper does. And don't even bother with the wait by the car thing." Cal spun around.

"Look, you can't go with us."

"Then I'll go out on my own."

"You can't do that."

"Watch me." He stalked out into the alley, wondering which way to head out. He saw the agents scatter in all directions. He didn't know which way to go.

TJ, you need to help me. I have to find Becky Lee and Scotty.

He'd no idea what made him ask TJ for help. That was just crazy talk.

But he was sure he was supposed to go to the left. Sure of it. He took off that direction at a steady lope.

Becky Lee bent over, catching her breath. She and Scotty were tucked way back in an entrance to another building, a few blocks from the warehouse where they'd been held. She didn't really know which way to go for help. Well, except for far away from where they'd been.

"Are we… safe?" Scotty gasped out his words, trying to catch his breath.

"We need to get further away. I need to find a way to call for help. I have no idea where we are."

"All the buildings are empty."

"Don't worry, we'll find someone to help us." Becky Lee just hoped it was soon. She peeked around the corner of the building. She saw a man walking quickly down the street in their direction. He glanced their way, looking up at that very moment and spied her. He sped up, running towards her. She grabbed Scotty's hand. "We have to go. Now."

They ran down the street, away from the man. She looked both directions, searching for a place to hide. She ducked into another alleyway but quickly saw her mistake. It was a dead end.

There wasn't enough time to retrace their steps without chancing the man catching up with them. She saw a stack of wooden crates piled high near the end of the alley. "This way."

As she started to run, Scotty stumbled. She turned to help him up. "Come on." She started running again.

"My shoe."

Becky Lee glanced back and saw Scotty's shoe in the alley where he'd stumbled. No time to get it. They needed to hide.

They raced to the end of the alley, and she tucked Scotty behind the crates and put herself in front of him, crouching low, hoping the man would run right past the alley.

She tried to settle her breath and listen. She pressed

her finger to her lips for Scotty to remain perfectly still. Footsteps echoed in the alley.

He'd found them.

Her heart pounded so hard in her chest it was a wonder the man couldn't hear it. He slowly made his way down the alley. She looked through a tiny slit between the crates and saw the man lean down and pick up Scotty's shoe.

"You can come out now. There's nowhere to run."

His footsteps came closer.

She had to think of something. There was no way she was letting the man take her and Scotty again. She watched him approach the stack of crates through the slit. Right as he got close she stood up and pushed on the stack of crates with all her might. They tumbled down on the man in a loud crash of splintering wood and shattering glass.

Scotty screamed.

She grabbed his hand and raced past the jumbled mess, hoping the man was pinned to the ground, or that it at least slowed him down and gave them time to find another place to hide.

CHAPTER 26

Cal heard Scotty scream. He broke into a full-out run in the direction of the scream, gasping for breath as he sprinted toward the noise. He had to get there. Protect them.

Just then he saw Becky Lee and Scotty come running around the corner. Becky Lee looked up and saw him. The relief was clear on her face as she raced towards him. His heart leapt in his chest, just at seeing them alive.

Becky Lee ran straight into his arms and he held her close while scooping up Scotty at the same time.

"We…. have… to run. He's after us." Becky Lee gasped each word.

Cal took a quick look around. "Over here." He pulled her into a doorway and grabbed his phone and started tapping in the agent's number. Before he could finish he saw two agents round the corner at full speed.

He stepped out of the doorway and they ran over to him.

"In that alley." Becky Lee pointed. "I toppled crates on top of the guy chasing us."

"Stay here," the agent ordered them.

Cal had no intention of going anywhere. He set Scotty down and looked him over from head to toe. "Are you okay?"

"Yep, but I *lost-ed* my shoe."

Cal was sure the way Scotty always added the extra syllable to lost was the most heart-wrenchingly adorable thing he'd ever heard. He looked down at the boy's feet. "Well, you sure did."

"You should have seen Aunt Becky. She saved us. We climbed out of a window. It was way high." Scotty flung his arm up. "But we made a tower and got out. Then we ran. But this guy chased us. So we hid behind this stuff in the alley. Then Aunt Becky pushed the stuff over on the man and smashed him."

Cal looked at Becky Lee., then at Scotty. He closed his eyes for a moment and opened them to make sure he wasn't dreaming, and they were both still standing there. He looked up at the sky and let out a huge breath.

Thanks for the help, TJ.

He looked at these two standing before him. They were his whole world. The ferocity of his emotions rocked him to his very core.

He loved them.

He loved Becky Lee.

He wasn't sure his legs could hold him any longer. The fear, the anger at his father, the relief at finding

Becky Lee and Scotty—and the sure knowledge that he was in love with Becky Lee—overwhelmed him.

He sank down on the step in the doorway and pulled Scotty and Becky Lee down beside him, tucking them both close to his side.

Cal sat with Scotty sheltered against his left side, and Becky Lee on his right. Scotty had his arms wrapped around Cal's arm, and Becky Lee had her hand resting on his knee.

The lead agent appeared in front of them. "We got the other kidnapper. He was just crawling out from under the crates. You're a very lucky woman."

"It wasn't luck so much as my sister was watching over us." Becky Lee eyed the agent with a look that dared him to doubt her.

"It appears your aunt is lucky now, too. With Luca arrested, the last of the Abelli family will be behind bars. They had a lot of enemies but hadn't made any alliances with other… *families*… in the last ten years or so. I'm thinking it's probably time for your aunt to come out of witness protection."

"Really?" Becky Lee jumped up. "She's free to come home?"

"That's the word from higher up the ranks than me."

"Cal, did you hear that? Aunt Ellie can come home."

Cal reached out a hand and pulled her back down beside him. "That is good news. But I'm not sure I can

235

stand to have you even five feet away from me. Sit down here with us again."

Becky Lee grinned. "Possessive man, aren't you?"

He hugged both Scotty and Becky Lee close. "I'm the luckiest man in the world right now, I know that much."

"So, how about you head over to see your father now? We could wrap all this up." Mr. I'm-in-Charge wouldn't let it rest.

"Go visit you father? What's he talking about?" Becky Lee looked up at him.

Cal sighed. "There is one more thing I need to do. I'm going to let these men take you back to Comfort Crossing. I have to deal with something. Something that should have been done long ago. I'm going to stop my father."

Becky Lee took his hand in hers and held it tightly. "You do what you need to do. We'll be waiting for you at home."

Cal hadn't been back to his childhood home in he didn't know how many years. They'd flown him to Chicago and gotten him a car. He'd thought that the agents would tape some kind of device on his chest or something, but all they'd done was give him a really nice watch. They said everything would be recorded on that. Then they'd taken his shirt, cut off a button, and sewed a new one on it. Some kind of camera transmitter. He felt like a futurist spy, but he was determined. No one messed with Becky Lee and Scotty and put them in danger like that. No one.

He drove up the long drive and stopped in front of the house. A mix of emotions swirled through him. Playing in the backyard with Gordon when they were boys. Being dressed up in suits and paraded in front of business associates at the many dinner parties his mother threw. Well, the staff threw the parties, but his mother took the credit. The house he'd longed to come home to when he was at boarding school.

Why was that?

He was taken better care of at school and had a handful of friends to keep him company. It was less lonely at boarding school than being at home.

He stepped out of the car, pushing aside his memories. He rang the doorbell, no longer feeling like he had a right to just walk into the house.

"Mr. James. We weren't expecting you."

Ah, his father's right-hand man was still on staff.

"Franklin." Cal nodded his head. "I need to see my father."

"I'll see if he's available. Wait here."

Cal stood inside the doorway and looked up at the long, winding stairway leading upstairs. The stairway with the banister that Gordon and he would slide down when their parents were gone. Always hiding their antics from their sister because she would always tell on them. Up those stairs and down a long hallway was his boyhood room, right next to Gordon's. A deep pain stabbed through him and nearly brought him to his knees.

He squared his shoulders. There was no time for memories. He was on a mission. For Becky Lee and Scotty. For Gordon. For all the people who his father had wronged.

His father stepped out of his office and into the hallway. "Wasn't expecting you."

"I need to talk to you."

"Come back here, then. I only have a few minutes."

Of course, only a few minutes. Who would want to spend more than that with his very own son?

He walked back to his father's office, the room he'd never been allowed in as a boy. The room was dark and very masculine, with a massive desk in the center of the room. His father motioned for him to sit down.

Cal stood.

"I'm not sure what we have to talk about. I'm not giving up trying for custody. I will get custody of the boy. I can't have him turning out like you and Gordon." His father stood behind the desk.

Cal balled his fist. "You're not going to get custody of Scotty."

"But I am."

"You're not the kind of man that Gordon would want raising his son."

"Gordon never knew what was good for himself, so, of course, he had no clue regarding his son. Scotty will be raised to be a Grayson. Work at the company."

Cal gritted his teeth at the callous way his father talked about Gordon. "You didn't even come to his funeral."

"Why would I? He made it clear he wanted nothing to do with me or the company."

"Because he was your *son*."

"Both my sons have been a grave disappointment to me."

"As you have been to your sons."

Cal's father's eyes flashed in anger, then turned icy cold. "I won't have you talking to me like that."

"I can talk to you however I want. I'm a grown man now."

His father laughed. "A grown man. No real job. No home. Nothing."

"I have Becky Lee and Scotty."

"You won't have the boy for long."

"You'll never get custody of him. Ever."

"I always get my way. One way or another."

"Well, your plan with the Abellis didn't work out so well." Cal caught a glimmer of surprise in his father's eyes.

"Don't know what you're talking about." His father picked up a letter from his desk and absently looked at it.

Cal knew that was a tell, what his father did when he was sorting something out in his mind. Quickly. Trying to stay one step ahead.

"Luca Abelli was arrested. For kidnapping Becky Lee and Scotty among other crimes. He'll never get out of prison now." Cal stepped up close to the desk. "I know you were working with him. Met with him."

"And if I did meet with him. What does that prove?"

"I know you well enough that it means you knew

what was going to happen. At the very least, you did nothing to stop it. You were probably even in on it."

"Prove it." His father set down the letter.

"I don't have to prove it. I know you were involved. You never let a little thing like laws and common decency get in your way. You are ruthless and… cruel."

"You are a weak man. Always disappointing me."

For the first time, his father's words didn't bother him. Didn't ring true. He no longer needed or wanted his approval. Nor cared what kind of expectations his father had had for him.

"No, despite all your attempts otherwise, Gordon and I turned out to be honest men. Happy, even."

"Gordon went to prison." His father stared him down.

"Because you set him up. And Gordon didn't have the heart to let his sister go to jail for what she'd done, not what he'd done."

"It was easier to let Gordon take the blame than lose Jillian. She's a wonder at the business. She just made an awkward mistake."

"So you let Gordon pay the price."

"It was a small price to pay. He wasn't going to amount to anything. He wasn't ever going to be able to take over the business like Jillian will. It was a choice I had to make. It was an easy choice. Gordon needed to take the fall. Jillian has been much more careful since then. A good lesson was learned by all."

"You let your son go to prison for something he didn't do."

"It was easy enough. Just had to have Tyson plant

some evidence. Like I said, Jillian was always proving herself and I couldn't afford to lose her then."

Tyson, his father's right-hand man. He'd been right, it was all his father's doing. "You are the worst father in the history of fathers," Cal spit out each word.

"You can't talk to me like that." His father slammed his palm on the desk. "You always were so impertinent."

"Well, you messed up on the Abelli, deal, didn't you? Didn't work out like you planned."

"The man was an idiot. He couldn't follow a plan if his life depended on it. It was all set up. The fool."

"I thought it was too well orchestrated to have been Abelli's plan."

"Of course, it wasn't his plan. The man is an imbecile. He couldn't follow my directions at all." His father's face reddened and he took a deep breath, calming himself.

His father plastered on a cheshire cat smile. "And yet, there is nothing to connect me with him. I made sure of that."

"What if Becky Lee or Scotty had been hurt?"

"I gave him strict orders that the boy wasn't to be harmed."

"But Becky Lee?"

"I really didn't trouble myself with what happened to her. Just the boy."

"That was very *caring* of you, Father." Cal stood and stared at his father for a moment or two, then he looked down at his watch and said slowly, "Do you have enough?"

"What are you talking about?" His father raised an eyebrow.

Cal heard a commotion in the hallway and the office door flew open. The lead agent stepped into the room flanked by two other agents and Franklin.

"I'm sorry, they just burst in, sir." Franklin shifted nervously.

"Mr. Grayson, you're under arrest." Mr. I'm-in-Charge walked over to the desk.

Cal was almost beginning to like the man. Maybe he should learn his name...

Cal's father shot him a deadly look. "You."

"Yes, Father. Me." He took off his watch and handed to an agent.

"What's going on?"

Cal turned and saw Jillian standing in the doorway.

"Ah, sister dear. I'm hoping that they have enough to arrest you, too. Or at least investigate more into Gordon's crime and exonerate him. It was a cowardly thing for you to let him take the blame for your actions."

Jillian walked into the room, her eyes blazing in anger. "What have you done, you foolish, foolish man?"

"I believe I've just made sure that justice is served." Cal pushed past his sister and walked out of his childhood home, sure he would never return.

CHAPTER 27

Cal arrived back in Comfort Crossing early the next morning. He stood in front of Becky Lee's home so full of gratitude that Becky Lee and Scotty hadn't been hurt. Anger at his father rushed through him again at all the man had done, what he had put his family through.

His family.

He thought of Becky Lee and Scotty as his family. A real one.

Becky Lee stepped out on the front porch. The morning sun lit her hair as she smiled at him. He bounded up the steps and took her in his arms.

"Welcome home." Becky Lee whispered.

He held her tight for a moment then stepped back. "Scotty okay?"

"He's still sound asleep. Poor kid was so exhausted."

"We don't have to worry about custody any more. My father won't ever be getting custody of Scotty."

Becky's eyes lit up. "Really?"

"They usually don't give custody to grandfathers who are in prison…"

"What?"

Before he'd time to explain it all to her, his cell phone rang. He thought of ignoring it, because he had everything he needed or wanted right here, but he dug it out of his pocket and answered it. "Hello?"

He listened to the voice on the other end of the phone and a huge grin crept across his face. He let out a whoop. "We'll be right there."

"What is it?" Becky Lee stood staring at him.

"It's TJ. She's awake."

Becky Lee held her breath as they stepped into Theresa Jean's room. Scotty rushed over to his mother's bedside.

"Mom?" His voice quavered.

Theresa Jean opened her eyes and smiled. "Hey, Scotty."

"You did wake up. You did. I knew you would. You've been sleeping forever, Mom."

Becky Lee and Cal walked up to the bed. Theresa Jean looked up at both of them. "How long?"

"Weeks." Becky Lee took her sister's hand in hers. "But the doctor says that things look good now. It will take some time to build your strength back."

Theresa Jean looked at Cal, her eyes searching his face. He nodded at her and one long tear trailed down Theresa Jean's cheek.

Becky Lee squeezed Theresa Jean's hand. "It's going to be okay. We're going to have you come back to Comfort Crossing while you get stronger. You can move in with me."

"Yes, Mom, Uncle Cal and I live with Aunt Becky now. They got married. And guess what. I have a dog now. Penny. She's awesome. You'll love her. I can keep her, right?"

Theresa Jean's eyes widened and she threw Becky Lee a questioning look.

"Yes, we're married. A long story best left for later. And Scotty has a dog now. She's adorable." There was no use tiring her sister, plenty of time to explain things later.

Theresa Jean licked her lips, and Becky Lee reached over for the glass of water, letting her sister slowly sip.

"Thanks." Theresa Jean looked at Scotty then at Cal. "Cal, your father?"

"He's not a problem anymore. Don't worry."

Theresa Jean closed her eyes. "I'm a bit tired."

"Scotty, why don't you say goodbye to your mom. We're going to let her rest. We'll come back tomorrow. As soon as she's ready, we'll move her home with us."

Scotty stood on tiptoe and kissed his mother's cheek. "Thanks for waking up, Mom. I bet you can't wait to meet Penny."

Becky Lee leaned over and kissed her sister's forehead. "Rest now. We'll be back."

Cal moved up to the head of the bed and leaned over and whispered something to Theresa Jean. Her sister opened her eyes briefly and smiled.

They walked out of the room and Becky Lee looked up at Cal. "What did you say to her?"

"I told her to hurry up and get strong enough to move to Comfort Crossing. And to make sure she brought lots of shoes. That Penny had just about chewed up all of yours…" He winked at her and followed Scotty down the hallway.

CHAPTER 28

G reta sat on the front porch reading a book. Or trying to read it. Her mind kept wandering. She took a sip of her tea and placed the book on the small table beside her chair. A bit of a breeze cooled her. Clay had installed a ceiling fan on the porch for her, and it stirred the air, making it comfortable to sit outside, even on warm summer evenings like this one.

She looked up as a car pulled into the driveway. It rolled to a stop, and both the driver's side door and the passenger side door opened. She watched as two people got out of the car.

Martin.

Ellie.

Greta stood up, her hand at her throat. Ellie hurried across the yard, up the steps, and threw her arms around Greta.

"Oh, Ellie. I never thought I'd see you again." Greta hugged her friend.

Martin climbed the steps and Greta held out a hand to him. A smile spread across his face.

"I thought you had to go back into hiding. What happened?"

"It's all behind us now. The Abellis are all in jail. I —*we*—don't have to hide anymore." Ellie's voice was low. "It is so strange to be back here after all these years. I never thought I'd see you, or Comfort Crossing ever again."

"You're both free now?" Greta stood in shock.

"Yes, we're free to come back here, live our lives." Martin grinned.

Ellie grabbed Martin's hands in hers. "I can never repay you for all you did for me. For all you gave up for me."

"Ah, Ellie, I'd do it again if I had to." Martin leaned over and kissed Ellie's cheek.

"I know you would. You're a good man and my best friend, but now it's time you took back your own life. I'm going to go see my brother now. I have a lot to explain to him. I can't wait to see my whole family." Ellie turned to leave. "I'll come back tomorrow and we'll talk, Greta. I've missed you so. We'll catch up on everything that's been going on in our lives."

"I'd like that."

"I'm leaving Martin here with you." Ellie grinned. "He's been waiting for this day for almost forty years."

Ellie returned to the car and drove off.

Greta stood with her mind racing at all that had happened in the last five minutes. Martin stepped up close, tilted her head up with one hand, and brushed back her hair with the other. "I have missed you so. It's like a piece of myself has been missing all these years."

Greta could barely take a breath. All this time. All the longing. All the wishing things had been different. Now here Martin was, standing right in front of her.

"Greta, I want you to give me a second chance. I need you to. Please. I've loved you for so many years. Can we please try again?"

Martin peered at her closely. "I guess I didn't even ask if you had someone in your life now."

"No, there's no one." Greta's voice came out in a whisper.

"Then will you give me another chance? I promise not to mess it up this time. I won't leave you. Can you trust me?"

Greta's heart skipped a beat and she looked up into the warm eyes of this man. The man she'd loved for so many years. "There is no second chance."

Martin's eyes widened, then traces of sadness darkened his face. "I don't blame you. I know I left you all those years ago. Told you I loved you, then left."

"That's not what I meant. There is no second chance because I never stopped loving you. You've always been in my heart. I do trust you. I know why you made your decision to leave before. But you're here now. That's all that matters."

Martin drew in a big gulp of air. "I do so love you, woman."

He leaned down and kissed her then. A long,

leisurely kiss that promised of days of love and time to get to know each other again.

"I love you, too. Always have. Always will."

∾

Cal moved back into the cottage next to Steve. TJ had taken his place in the sunroom at Becky Lee's. He missed getting up each morning and having breakfast with Becky Lee and Scotty, missed sitting on the porch at night, talking about their days. He still went over every day to check on TJ and Scotty—and Becky Lee— but it wasn't the same.

TJ got stronger every day and made noises about finding her own place for herself and Scotty. But that wouldn't matter either. Becky Lee had married him to keep Scotty safe, not because she was in love with him. She even kept hinting that it was time for him to move on, and how much she knew he loved to wander from town to town and job to job.

Only he didn't want that anymore. He wanted what he couldn't have. He wanted to be married to Becky Lee for real, because she loved him, because she wanted him —not because she wanted to keep Scotty safe.

Cal took a swig of his beer and continued painting the wall at the cottage. He'd promised Steve he'd be all finished with the work soon. He turned up some music on the stereo in the corner, hoping to chase his thoughts away by the loud songs.

That didn't work.

He finally gave up, washed the paint brush, and

went to sit on the front porch. Louie came running over. "Hey, buddy." Cal leaned over and stroked the dog.

Steve came wandering over after Louie. "Sorry about that. Louie is bored. Josh is spending the night at a friend's house."

"Louie is always welcome. It's nice to have company."

"Then do you mind if I grab a beer and join you?"

"Not at all."

Steve disappeared into the cottage, came back with a beer, and dropped into a chair beside Cal. "Heat wave is supposed to break tomorrow."

"Is it? Good. We could use some cooler weather."

Steve took a long swig of beer. "Listen, it's none of my business, so you can tell me to butt out, but why are you living here? Away from Becky Lee? I know you guys got married suddenly, but I thought things were working out okay. You always looked so happy around her."

Cal sighed. "I was happy. It's complicated. We got married for… various reasons."

"You mean to improve your chances of keeping custody of Scotty?"

Cal looked at Steve in surprise. "You knew that?"

"I figured it was why you two hurried up and got married. But I also thought I saw you fall in love with her as time went along."

Cal stared out into the distance. "I did. Which is why things are so… wrong now. She married to keep Scotty safe, not because she loves me."

"Well, have you told her that you love her?" Steve stared at Cal over the top of his beer bottle.

"No, I mean, why would I? That wasn't part of our agreement. Now Scotty is safe. There is no reason for her to stay married to me. What do I have to offer her anyway? I've moved around for years. I don't even know how to be a husband. Or have a family. Look at the mess I came from. My father almost got Becky Lee killed." Cal raked his hand through his hair. "I have nothing to offer her."

"I don't know, buddy. You have the strongest, most important thing in the world to give her."

"What's that?"

"Love." Steve finished his beer, set the bottle down, and whistled for Louie. "Think about it."

Cal watched Steve and Louie walk back to their house. He saw Holly pull into Steve's drive and get out of her car. Steve wrapped her in his arms and kissed her. Envy skittered through Cal. It was so easy for Steve and Holly.

But he just wasn't sure that Steve was right. Was loving Becky Lee enough for her?

"Um, that's nice" Holly kissed Steve back then pulled back and looked at him. "What's wrong?"

"What do you mean? Nothing's wrong."

"You have that troubled look about your eyes."

Steve laughed and pulled her close. "You can read me like a book."

"So?"

"Oh, I was just over talking to Cal. The man is in love with Becky Lee."

"And that's a problem, why?"

"They rushed into marriage to help Cal keep custody of Scotty."

"I thought as much."

Steve took Holly's hand and led her onto the porch. "But now Cal has gone and fallen in love with Becky Lee."

"Has he told her?"

"Exactly what I asked. He hasn't."

"Well, he should."

"I know. But he says since Becky Lee married him just because of Scotty, he doesn't feel right changing the agreement up now."

"That's ridiculous. Besides, I saw Becky Lee and Cal together the other day. I'm pretty certain that Becky Lee is nuts about him." Holly shook her head.

"The two of them need to talk, then."

"They do. Let's hope they talk before it's too late."

"You've been kind of moping around this last week. What's up?" Theresa Jean sat on a park bench next to Becky Lee while they watched Scotty, Josh, and the two dogs play.

"I don't know. I just feel… out of sorts."

"You know what the problem is, don't you?"

"No." Becky Lee pursed her lips. "What is the problem?"

"You miss him."

"Who?"

"Don't be dense. Cal. You miss him."

Becky Lee sighed. "I do miss him a bit. I got used to having him around. I was teaching him to cook a few things. At least I don't have to worry about him starving, he can feed himself now."

"So you miss him *a bit*?"

"Okay, okay. I miss him a lot. I wasn't prepared to miss him, that's all. Besides, he just married me to keep Scotty safe, not because he cared about me."

"You're a dope sometimes, you know that, sis?"

"What do you mean?"

"It's obvious that you're in love with the man."

"I am not." Becky Lee sat back. "Am I?"

Her sister laughed. "Does your heart flutter when you see him? Do you miss sharing all the little details of your day? Heck, do you miss his kisses?"

"Yes." Becky Lee sighed. "Yes to all of the above."

Theresa Jean's eyes saddened. "Well, there is one thing I've learned. Life is short. You need to take every opportunity for happiness. You never know when someone you love might be taken away from you."

Becky Lee gave her sister a hug. "I'm sorry. I know you miss Gordon."

"I do. So much that sometimes I feel like I can't breathe." Theresa Jean looked directly into Becky Lee's eyes. "So, I guess I don't understand why you won't take a chance, risk telling Cal you love him. You might never get another opportunity and you'll wonder all your life 'what if.'"

Becky Lee looked at Theresa Jean, a woman wise beyond her years. The thing was, Becky Lee didn't know which she was more scared of—telling Cal she loved him or risking him leaving her for good.

CHAPTER 29

Cal stood in the corner of Greta's yard. Greta had thrown a big barbecue to welcome her friend Ellie back home. She'd invited what looked to be at least half the town. Becky Lee and her friends, Jenny and Bella, and their husbands. TJ and Scotty. Gil Amaud and his girlfriend. He couldn't remember her name, he'd have to ask Becky Lee.

He could use that as an excuse to talk to her. Becky Lee was surrounded by her friends and family. It was easy to see she belonged here. He felt more and more like the outsider.

"Uncle Cal." Scotty and Penny came loping up to him. "You should come over here and see this." Scotty grabbed his hand and tugged on him.

"Okay, okay, I'm coming."

"Let me get Mom and Aunt Becky." Scotty raced over and pulled the two women over to where Cal stood under the tree.

"Hey TJ, Becky Lee." He shifted uncomfortably, then leaned against the tree. He wasn't quite certain, but he thought TJ rolled her eyes.

"Watch this." Scotty's face turned all serious. "Penny, sit."

The dog sat.

"Penny, shake."

The dog raised a paw for Scotty to shake.

"Penny, high five."

Cal laughed when Penny put both her paws in Scotty's hand.

"Now watch this." Scotty took a step back. "Penny, say yes."

The dog bobbed her head up and down.

"That's great, kiddo. You've really been working with him." Cal smiled at Scotty.

"You know what? I think that deserves an ice cream cone. Why don't you come with me and we'll find one." TJ took the boy's hand, started walking away and turned back for a moment. She shrugged her shoulders, and this time he was sure she rolled her eyes at him.

Cal screwed up his courage and took Becky Lee's hand in his. His heart pounded and he swallowed. Then swallowed again. "I need to talk to you."

"Okay." She looked up at him with her fathomless blue eyes.

"I know we got married because of Scotty." He closed his eyes for a second, then opened them. "But somewhere along the line, I fell in love with you. Totally and completely. I can't imagine my life without you in it. I don't know that I can live up to your expectations of what a husband should be. I know this isn't what you agreed to, what you planned on when you said you'd marry me—"

Becky Lee held up a finger to his lips, stopping him. "I love you, too."

Cal's whole world just dropped into place like the last piece on one of Scotty's jigsaw puzzles. "You love me?"

"I do."

He leaned down and kissed her gently, his finger threading through her hair. "I've been wanting to do that for weeks."

"I've been wanting you to do that for weeks." Becky Lee grinned back at him.

Cal took a step back and dropped to one knee. "Becky Lee, will you stay married to me? I love you and want to spend the rest of our lives together."

Tears filled Becky Lee's eyes. "I'd like nothing more than to stay married to you."

Cal got back up to his feet and wrapped his arms around her. "You know what else?"

"What?"

"I think we should have a proper wedding night." He winked at her.

Becky Lee broke into one of her captivating smiles —the ones that made his heart flip in his chest—and reached up to touch his face. "I think it's about time you move back in… and this time, none of that sunroom nonsense. You should move right into my bedroom."

"I'd like nothing better in this whole wide world." He leaned down and pressed one more kiss to her lips.

He realized he could do that anytime he wanted now. No reason to wait for someone to be watching them. No reason to wait at all.

So he didn't.

He kissed her again.

ALSO BY KAY CORRELL

THANK YOU for reading my story. I hope you enjoyed it. Sign up for my newsletter to be updated with information on new releases, promotions, and give-aways. The signup is at my website, kaycorrell.com.

Reviews help other readers find new books. I always appreciate when my readers take time to leave an honest review.

I love to hear from my readers. Feel free to contact me at authorcontact@kaycorrell.com

COMFORT CROSSING ~ THE SERIES

The Shop on Main - Book One

The Memory Box - Book Two

The Christmas Cottage - A Holiday Novella (Book 2.5)

The Letter - Book Three

The Christmas Scarf - A Holiday Novella (Book 3.5)

The Magnolia Cafe - Book Four

The Unexpected Wedding - Book Five

The Wedding in the Grove (crossover short story between series - Josephine and Paul from The Letter.)

LIGHTHOUSE POINT ~ THE SERIES

Wish Upon a Shell - Book One

Wedding on the Beach - Book Two

Love at the Lighthouse - Book Three

ABOUT THE AUTHOR

Kay Correll writes stories that are a cross between contemporary romance and women's fiction. She likes her books with a healthy dose of happily ever after. Her stories are set in the fictional small towns of Comfort Crossing, Mississippi and Belle Island, Florida. While her books are a series, each one can be read as a stand-alone story.

Kay lives in the Midwest of the U.S. and can often be found out and about with her camera, taking a myriad of photographs which she likes to incorporate into her book covers. When not lost in her writing or photography, she can be found spending time with her ever-supportive husband, knitting, or playing with her puppies—two cavaliers and one naughty but adorable Australian shepherd. Kay and her husband also love to travel. When it comes to vacation time, she is torn between a nice trip to the beach or the mountains—but the mountains only get considered in the summer—she swears she's allergic to snow.

Learn more about Kay and her books at kaycorrell.com

While you're there, sign up for her newsletter to hear about new releases, sales, and giveaways.

WHERE TO FIND ME:
kaycorrell.com
authorcontact@kaycorrell.com